Virginie Grimaldi was born in Bordeaux where she still lives. Translated into more than twenty languages, her novels are carried by endearing characters and a poetic and sensitive pen. She is the most read French novelist in 2019, 2020 and 2021 (*Le Figaro littéraire/GFK* awards) and the winner of the Favourite Book of the French in 2022 (*France Télévisions*). She is the author of *Chasing the Stars*, *How to Find Love in the Little Things*, and *A Good Life* (Europa Editions, 2024).

Hildegarde Serle graduated in French from Oxford University. After working as a newspaper subeditor in London for many years, she obtained the Chartered Institute of Linguists Diploma in Translation. For Europa she has translated Christelle Dabos' Mirror Visitor series and the novels by Valérie Perrin, including the bestselling *Fresh Water for Flowers*.

Dear reader,

Welcome to the home of Jeanne, Iris and Théo. I hope you'll feel at home here, too.
Thank you for reading my book!
Yours,
Virginie Grimaldi

ALSO BY

VIRGINIE GRIMALDI

A Good Life

Virginie Grimaldi

ALL THAT REMAINS

*Translated from the French
by Hildegarde Serle*

Europa Editions
8 Blackstock Mews
London N4 2BT
www.europaeditions.co.uk

This book is a work of fiction. Any references to historical events,
real people, or real locales are used fictitiously.

Copyright © Librairie Arthème Fayard, 2022
First publication 2025 by Europa Editions

Translation by Hildegarde Serle
Original title: *Il nous restera ça*
Translation copyright © 2025 by Europa Editions

All rights reserved, including the right of reproduction
in whole or in part in any form.

A catalogue record for this title is available from the British Library
ISBN 978-1-78770-563-0

Grimaldi, Virginie
All That Remains

Cover design by Ginevra Rapisardi

Cover illustration by Valérie Renaud

Prepress by Grafica Punto Print – Rome

The authorized representative in the EEA
is Edizioni e/o, via Gabriele Camozzi 1, 00192 Rome, Italy.

Printed and bound in Great Britain by Clays Ltd, Elcograf S.p.A

CONTENTS

Prologue - 15

September - 25

October - 57

November - 93

December - 121

January - 171

February - 211

Epilogue - 253

Acknowledgments - 257

For Serena, Sophie, and Cynthia,
my certainties.

There is a crack in everything
That's how the light gets in
—Leonard Cohen

One mustn't be afraid of happiness
It's just a good time to be had
—Romain Gary

ALL THAT REMAINS

Prologue

Jeanne
Three months earlier

It was the big day. Jeanne hadn't slept a wink all night. She tidied her chignon and pinned the veil onto it. Her hands were shaking a little, making the task trickier. She'd insisted on getting ready alone, despite everyone's persistent offers of support. She knew the importance of this moment, the kind of turning point that lodges deep in the memory, never to depart, and she wanted to engage fully with it, with no distractions. Through the window, the June sun dappled the room's oak floorboards. This golden pool was her favorite spot in the apartment. It would appear late morning, when the sun's rays found their way between the chimney stacks of the building opposite. Jeanne liked nothing more than just to stand there, both feet planted in the gentle warmth. One day, Pierre had caught her in the act, facing the window, eyes closed, arms outstretched, bathed in sunlight. Stark naked. She'd wanted to disappear between the floorboards, so mortified was she, but Pierre had laughed:

"I've always dreamt of marrying a meerkat."

It was an improbable, original, almost crazy marriage proposal. The fourth since they'd moved in together. She'd turned down all the others, being passionate about freedom. But there, in that pool of light, seduced by the eccentricity of this man who accepted her own eccentricity, she had said yes.

The clock in the sitting room chimed, she was late. Jeanne did a final quick check in the mirror and left the apartment.

She had decided to walk to the church, a couple of streets away. On the way, several eyes lingered on her. Some heads turned. A young girl filmed her with her phone. Her outfit didn't go unremarked. Jeanne noticed none of it, preoccupied with but one thought: in a few minutes she would be with Pierre. He should already be there, in the fine gray suit she had chosen.

The church forecourt was empty. Everyone was inside. Jeanne smoothed down the fabric of her long dress while trying to control her shaking. Her legs could barely support her. She stuck a smile on her face and walked through the wooden doors.

The church was packed. The pews hadn't sufficed, so chairs had been added alongside, and several people remained standing. All eyes turned to Jeanne. She paid no attention. Slowly, she walked up the aisle without ever taking her eyes off Pierre. For a moment, she wondered if her chest could withstand the pounding of her heart. Some music she didn't know came from the organ, and yet she'd requested Leonard Cohen's "Hallelujah." The priest was standing behind the altar, hands joined.

To her right, a movement caught Jeanne's attention. Suzanne was indicating an empty seat to her, in the front pew. She smiled, and continued on her path towards the man she loved.

The organ stopped when she reached him. The silence was total. Jeanne gazed at Pierre's face for a long time. His full lashes, his rounded chin, his straight forehead. She had never tired of his features. They had become her landscape, her scenery. How could she do without them? The priest cleared his throat, the service would have to begin. She gave him a weak smile, thinking back to Father Maurice who had married them in this very church fifty years ago, and then lifted her black veil, leant over the coffin and, on her husband's lips, planted their final kiss.

Théo
Two months earlier

I've found an old car. A guy came into the bakery to ask if his ad could be pinned up. I was busy icing the coffee éclairs.

He said to Nathalie: "It's urgent, I need cash."

She said no, she hates paper cluttering the counter, always turns away anyone wanting to leave ads or notices. The guy was already on the sidewalk when I caught up with him. He had a face you'd be more likely to run from than trust, with a twitching eye, and paws the size of rackets, but while he needed cash, I needed four wheels.

He was waiting for me in the parking lot at closing time. Going by the price, I was expecting the worst, but it was worse than the worst. A white 205 with a smashed-in fender, and the rest no better. On hood and trunk, he'd swapped the Peugeot badges for Ferrari ones. The back window was plastered with the classiest of stickers. I asked to take a look at the engine, the hood just wouldn't open. But the car started, and that's all that mattered.

"I'll give you a hundred euros for it," I said.

"Three hundred, non-negotiable," he replied.

"It won't keep going for long, it's not worth three hundred."

His eye twitched faster, maybe he was threatening me in Morse code.

"I said 'non-negotiable,' don't waste my time. D'you want it, or not?"

I walked around the car again, checked out the seats, they were in quite good shape.

"Two hundred and a coffee éclair. That's all I've got, bro."

He looked down, and I took the chance to glance at his hands. I shouldn't have. With one slap, he'd send me into space. He held one out to me:

"Deal. Keep the éclair, I'm on a diet."

He amended the registration papers and we filled in the sales forms. He recounted the bills twice, then stuffed them into the inside pocket of his bomber jacket. A third of my first wages. Before leaving, he gave me a slap on the back; my arm nearly fell off. I threw my bag on the back seat, stuck on the P plate, and sped off.

The roads in Paris are jam-packed, the car stalls at every red light. It's the first time I'm driving since getting my license. Here, I get around on the metro.

Tomorrow, I'll have worked for two months. At school, the teachers encouraged me to pursue my studies. But I no longer had the choice. With the vocational training certificate, I earn almost half the minimum wage. At the bakery, they warned me: don't count on a permanent contract once you've got your diploma. But in this business, there's no shortage of work. I'm skilled: where I used to live, everyone loved my cakes. They'd ask me to bake them for every occasion, and I didn't need to be asked twice. They must miss them.

There's honking behind me. In the rear-view mirror, a guy's shouting at me. I turn the key, press on the accelerator, the car splutters, I try again, it starts just as the lights turn amber. I move forward, with a little wave for the guy in the rear-view mirror. He responds with his middle finger.

I arrive in Montreuil just as the darkness does. I find a parking space in Rue Condorcet, opposite a small house with blue shutters. I reach for my bag and take out the sandwich that Nathalie sold me. Two euros because it was destined for the trash can. She sighed when I asked if I could pay for it tomorrow. She's so tight, I bet she uses both sides of the toilet paper.

Rain starts to fall, I test the windshield wipers, they don't work. I don't care. I don't intend to drive around in this car. I settle down on the back seat, head resting on my bag, covered with my coat. I put in my earbuds and play Grand Corps Malade's latest song. I light the roll-up saved since this morning and close my eyes. It's a long time since I've felt this good. No sleeping in the metro for me tonight. For 200 euros, I've treated myself to a home.

Iris
One month earlier

At two years old, I fell off the wooden horse of a carousel. My father hadn't secured me properly and was distracted by my mother calling out to him, from a bench, to hold me. I broke my wrist and had to have surgery and stitches. My mother blamed my father, my father blamed my mother, I blamed the horse. That was my first scar.

At six years old, so as to impress my cousin, I gave my all in a race across my grandmother's parquet floor on cloth "skates." My bottom lip split open, like the parting of the Red Sea. At the hospital, they closed it up with sticky tape. That was my second scar.

At seven years old, my neighbors' apricot-colored poodle went off with a piece of my calf. That was my third scar.

At eleven years old, during an English class, I'd just been asked a question by the teacher when a sharp pain made me double up. Thinking it was a ruse to avoid my turn, she refused to let me go to the infirmary. The following morning, I was having my appendix removed, and, thanks to her guilt, I became my English teacher's pet. That was my fourth scar.

At seventeen years old, I had a mole removed from my cheek. It was raised and ugly—like having a Coco Pop stuck on my face. I needed five anesthetic injections and six stitches. That was my fifth scar.

At twenty-two years old, I got up one morning with a pain around my coccyx that forced me to walk as if wearing flippers. Upon examination, the doctor found an abscess that required immediate surgery. The anesthesia didn't work properly, I thought I was dying, but when I came round, the ceiling reassured me that I wasn't in heaven. For three weeks, I had a thick dressing perfectly positioned to cushion my backside. That was my sixth scar.

At twenty-six years old, thanks to a gust of wind while sunbathing on the beach, I got whacked on the shin by my towel-neighbor's parasol stand. He apologized profusely and took the chance to invite me to dinner. I thought it better to leave with the paramedics. That was my seventh scar.

At thirty years old, I met Jérémy. That's my eighth scar.

September

1
JEANNE

Jeanne plunged the blender into the pan and watched the flesh of the vegetables disintegrate.

Over fifty years, she and Pierre had woven their habits together. It was she who woke first, driven from sleep by her dark thoughts. She was born that way, with an oppressive melancholy that shrouded all good news and joyous moments. Sometimes, for no apparent reason, she would feel a chasm opening in the pit of her stomach and a huge void sucking her down. She'd gotten used to it, like one does a background noise.

She would get out of bed quietly, make herself some tea, and settle down in the second room, where she'd sew until Pierre, in turn, got up. Then they would breakfast together, get ready together, and leave together for their separate workplaces. In the evening, she would get home after him, he'd have been to the bakery, she to the grocery, and they would cook together, dine together, watch a movie or TV program together.

For the past three months, Jeanne had been unweaving those habits, thread by thread. The plural had become singular. The setting was the same, the timing the same, and yet everything rang hollow. Even the melancholy had disappeared, as if her entire life had been training for the bereavement she was now facing. She was desensitized.

Boudine barked when the doorbell rang. The mailman was standing at the door, holding a registered letter.

"Signature please, Madame Perrin."

She obliged, while Boudine eagerly sniffed the man's shoes. This dog's particular talent was to imitate perfectly a pig's grunt.

Jeanne didn't open the envelope, she knew what it contained.

The same as the two previous envelopes. She hadn't answered the last phone call, either. It was Pierre who took care of the bank accounts. She knew, because he'd not hidden it from her, that the financial situation had been precarious for several months.

Jeanne and Pierre belonged to what was called the middle class. Their salaries had allowed them to become the owners, in 1969, of a four-room apartment in the 17th arrondissement, and to live reasonably well, without great excess or hardship. Once a year, they treated themselves to a trip abroad, and donated to several charities. Retirement had curbed their lifestyle, they had vacationed closer to home, reduced how much fish and meat they ate, and Pierre had applied himself to doing the accounts more regularly. The widow's pension Jeanne now received instead of Pierre's pension had made their bank account plummet into the red. The banking adviser, although sympathetic, had suggested that she sell her apartment. That was out of the question. It wasn't *her* apartment, it was *their* apartment. Pierre still lived there, in the pipe-tobacco smell that had seeped into the walls, in the kitchen door he'd painted green one spring day, in his stooped silhouette she could still make out at the window.

She placed the envelope on the hall sideboard, and then let Boudine jump onto her knees. She switched on the TV and picked a random channel. Anything rather than the silence. On the screen, a young man was showing people around the rooms of an apartment. A voice, presumably that of the reporter, was giving the statistics for what he said was a booming rental sector. A banner headline summed it up: "Apartment sharing—a winning formula."

2
THÉO

Like every Thursday, it's the garbage truck that wakes me. It's 6 A.M. I sink my head back into the pillow I swiped from Monoprix. They didn't notice a thing, I went in with a flat stomach, and left on the verge of giving birth. I wasn't picky, I took the cheapest pillow. I had to—on the first night, I'd slept against my bag and got a stiff neck that was off the scale. My head was stuck facing left, impossible to straighten up, forced to walk with chassé steps, like some kind of "Lame-Swan Lake." And yet I'm not that fussy about sleeping arrangements, I'm used to crashing out anywhere. The metro was the worst, not because of the tiling, but because of the fear. Once time, three guys grabbed me to nab my phone, I thought I'd had it. I'm much better off in my jalopy.

Like every morning, I check social media. I've a message from Gérard, I don't open it. Nothing else. Didn't take them long to forget me.

The blue-shuttered house is still sleeping. I like imagining life inside it. At school, the teachers criticized me for having my head in the clouds, called me the dreamer. I don't dream, I escape. Reality is my prison.

Behind those blue shutters, I imagine wall-to-wall carpets. Soft, so your feet really sink in, not scratchy like I had in my room. A vanilla aroma, candles glowing. Background music, classical, or some such. Keys on the hall table, slippers beneath it. A steaming cup of coffee on the low table. The mother on the sofa, still in pajamas, reading a Romain Gary novel for the fifth time. The father in the shower, whistling a tune. The son still asleep, between a plump duvet and a pillow that wasn't stolen.

A cat purring on its master's tummy. Shit. My imagination's a Christmas TV movie.

I'm trying to motivate myself to get up and get dressed. Every evening, I get undressed before crashing, and cover myself with the old coat Ahmed gave me when I left. I do a wash every fortnight at the Red Cross social laundromat. I brush my teeth with water from a flask, and for the rest, I use the sink at the bakery during lunch break. Twice a week, I have a free shower at the municipal baths, and a quick shave. I've always hated being grubby, can't bear it when I stink—a hot shower every day is what I miss the most. That, and people to matter to.

I'm still dozing when a light dazzles me. A fist bangs on the car, I soon realize it's the cops. I open the door—the handles to lower the windows are missing.

"Police, papers please."

I feel like responding "scissors," but not sure it'd make them laugh.

There's two of them, friendly enough, they explain that I have to leave. I'm at twelve parking tickets in two months; despite regularly moving the car a few spaces along, it's not enough.

"You can't stay here."

I explain that I'm doing no harm, that I just want to have a quiet rest, that every morning I take line 9 to go to work, and come back at night to sleep, but it's no good, they want me gone.

"Why do you stick to this street?" the youngest of the two asks me.

I shrug. They carry on talking, threaten to get the car towed away, but I've stopped listening. Behind them, on the second floor, a blue shutter is just opening.

3
Iris

It's the twelfth apartment I've seen. Seedier than the eleven others, and yet no sure thing. The real-estate agent doesn't even bother to open his mouth, the market does his work for him: there are about twenty of us, crammed on the landing and down the stairs, each with the ultimate desire of writing our name on the scruffy doorbell. The rent is obscenely high, and yet I hear a young woman offering to pay more. A bearded guy complains loudly, the others, including me, choose not to rock the boat, to avoid our applications being thrown out. Surreptitiously, I observe them, trying to gauge, from appearance and attitude, what their salary is. How many have a superior application file to mine? Nineteen, without any doubt.

Since I've been in Paris, my savings have melted away. The studio I rent by the week costs me less than a hotel, but I won't be able to keep this up for long.

The agent closes the door of the hovel and puts all our forms into his bag:

"We're going to look closely at the documentation, and I'll keep you posted."

I rush down the stairs, leaving my hopes on the sixth floor. He won't call me. I don't work full time, no one can be a guarantor for me, I'm missing certain papers. I don't know why I go to these viewings. I've got more chance of finding a notorious fugitive than finding an apartment.

I stop off at the grocery store to buy something for supper. Like every evening, I'll be eating tête-à-tête with a screen.

My neighbor across the landing opens his door as I pass. I

do try not to make any noise, but this man's hearing is as good as his breath is bad, and that's saying something.

"Who are you?"

"I'm renting the studio for a few days, I already saw you this morning."

"Got anything to drink?"

"I should have a drop of orange juice left."

He roars with laughter:

"Took me for a queer, did you?"

My key has, of course, sunk to the bottom of my bag. I rummage through everything, in vain. The neighbor won't let me go, I hear him moving closer.

"And to smoke, got nothing either?"

"Sorry, I don't smoke."

"So, my neighbor's a goody two-shoes!" he shouts out to the entire stairwell.

While his sarcasm continues, my fingers finally touch metal. I clutch the key and turn it in the lock, before shutting the door in the neighbor's face.

Once safely out of his sight and hearing, I summon up my courage, stand facing the closed door, raise my chin, puff out my chest, and whisper my finest put-down:

"Get back in your cave, Neanderthal."

4
JEANNE

"I did the accounts, and it's not looking good."

Jeanne tilted the watering can to moisten the soil around the diplodenia. New, deep-pink flowers kept appearing, despite the gloomy forecast. Fall was at the gate. She'd never relished this time of year—it tolled the knell for fine days and rolled out the red carpet for the dead season. But, for the first time, the approach of October didn't sadden her. She had got through July and August with total indifference, and hadn't sought to cling on to summer. Now, all months had the same flavor.

"I know you're laughing away, you must think I'm joking, but I've never been so serious: I did the accounts. Miracles do happen. I spent precisely four hours and twelve minutes on them, and the verdict is final: I'm short of two hundred euros to get me to the end of the month, and that's after cutting spending to a strict minimum."

Jeanne pulled a cloth out of her bag and started wiping the plaques. Slowly, gently, she dusted the engraved letters. "To our teacher"; "To our beloved uncle"; "To my love, for evermore." As she did every day, she kept the photo screwed onto the headstone until last. She stroked his forehead, his eyes, his mouth, summoning the feel of his skin beneath her fingers. It was at once the sweetest moment and the most painful. These few seconds with him were worth the cruel disillusionment that would follow.

"You're going to gloat hearing it, but you were right. We should have put money aside. You always were more careful than me."

Jeanne's acute awareness that humans are finite had one virtue: she had both feet firmly planted in the here and now. She tackled tomorrow at dawn, not before. When Pierre would talk of saving for their old age, it was like a foreign language to her.

"And what if I die before you?" he would often fret. "Your salary isn't very high, your pension will be next to nothing. How will you manage?"

"You'd just better not," she would, invariably, retort. "Must I remind you that I'm three months older than you?"

Jeanne folded the cloth and sat down on the nearby bench. Boudine stretched out at her feet. The wind made a weeping willow's branches shiver. She wondered whether having that particular tree in the cemetery had been a deliberate choice.

"I never thought that, one day, you wouldn't be here anymore," she murmured.

She remained there a long time, telling Pierre all she could tell him. She exhausted the topics, stretched them out until they lost all substance. And yet that was her husband's habit, cluttering up his stories with superfluous details. How often had she switched off while he was talking to her? Jeanne's parents had taught her only to open her mouth when it was strictly necessary. And here she was, at seventy-four, telling a gravestone about the TV program on the dangers of sugar that she'd watched the previous day. She would have recited the telephone directory if doing so gave her an excuse to stay longer. Their conversations were, without doubt, what she missed the most. She liked sharing her thoughts with him as much as debating social issues. He was the person who knew her the best, understood her the best. He would anticipate her reactions, gauge her state of mind. When they were watching a movie and a scene really moved her—often when a birth or a baby featured—she would see, out of the corner of her eye, Pierre's head turning in her direction. Then, by resting his hand on her thigh, he would show her that he knew, and was there. How was she going to endure life without him?

Daylight was fading when she rose from the bench. She walked the few meters separating her from her husband, and then laid her hand on his photo.

"I'll be back tomorrow, my love. I'll have found a solution."

When she got home, Jeanne picked up her mail. She had received a letter, which she opened without thinking, once inside her flat. It was a text printed on a sheet of white paper.

Winter 1980

Pierre can't ease Jeanne's grief. At thirty-seven, she's become an orphan. Her mother has just died after battling cancer for two long years. Her father had only just preceded her, carried off by a heart attack in his early sixties. At the funeral, Jeanne and her sister, Louise, hold hands like when they were children. Jeanne's life goes on, she leaves every morning to work in the atelier, comes home every evening, back to her Pierre, but sadness has erased her sweet smile. Pierre tries everything to cheer her up. He takes her to the theater, to the movies, to the Basque Country, but she remains inconsolable. One day, he has an idea. His idea has four paws, a long body, and floppy ears. It was love at first sight for both the dog and Jeanne. She decides to call it Saucisse and smiles for the first time in weeks.

Jeanne's legs were giving way. Her heart was pounding. She slumped onto the sofa and reread the letter twice. It wasn't signed. A label printed with her name and address had been stuck on the envelope.

The contents of the letter were astonishingly—and worryingly—accurate. Who could have sent it to her? All those who knew this story were no longer part of her life, in one way or another.

It disturbed her so much that she had to go and lie down for a while. During the few seconds it had taken to read the letter, the past had risen to the surface. With disturbing realism, she had again seen Pierre walking through the door with a dog in his arms. He'd been late coming home from work, she'd been worried. The death of her parents had made her feel vulnerable:

she expected all those she loved to disappear. Pierre hadn't said a word. He had seemed apprehensive of her reaction. He had bent down and placed the little creature on the floor. That sausage-like body, that wagging tail, the sound of those claws on the floorboards, and that nose sniffing at everything in its path had all banished her slight misgivings. Pierre had muttered to her: "A client wanted to part with it. I thought it would need love, and you could give it the love you've now got to spare." It was one of her happiest moments in a long time.

5
Théo

I've signed up to Tinder. Don't know what came over me, always said I'd never join a dating app. I don't believe in love that much, but it's like with God, I hope, one day, someone will prove me wrong.

So, I was in the car, questioning things, like I do every evening, while staring at the inside light. Why we're here, what the point of living is since we're going to die, why I didn't end up in another family, does a fridge light go out when you close the door. And I felt even more lonely than usual, and yet what's usual is already peak loneliness.

At the bakery, Nathalie listens to Radio Nostalgie, and it's worthy of its name—all day long, it's dead people singing about life. This afternoon, there was a program on dating apps, and loads of people phoned in to say they'd found the love of their life that way. Which is probably why, with only loneliness for company this evening, I signed up.

I posted the only photo of me I like, seen from the back, watching the sun setting. Manon took it, we'd just arrived at Seignosse, hopped off the bus and run to the beach. It was the first time I was seeing the sea.

Once I've filled in all my details, the photos of girls start rolling in. At first, it's amusing. There are those who post pics of themselves laughing or doing sport, those who smile shyly, who overuse filters, who pose with their cat, who are never without their girlfriends, who try to appear melancholic. I play the game and stick a green heart on some of them, pretty randomly. Sometimes, I crack up laughing, like with "Marie," who has exactly the same look and expression on all the photos, it's freaky—like she's just changed the scenery or her outfit. Or with "Jenny65," who's clearly blind drunk on a sofa, bottle in mouth, like some skit on YouTube. But all in all, the site doesn't do much for me. I feel like I'm looking for the coolest cap on a dull clothing site. Maybe it's because I'm not a looker, and know that appearance isn't everything, maybe it's because Manon still lurks in my mind, I don't know, but the site makes me uneasy. I feel even more lonely just thinking about all those lonely people on the other side of the screen. I'm about to close the app when a message appears: I've got a match. A girl I'd "liked" has "liked" me, too.

Out of curiosity, I click open the window. Her handle's "Bella," she's eighteen. A photo of feet in the sand. A message tells me I can chat with her. I think very quickly. I've never done this. The first sentence doesn't matter if I never meet her, but suppose she's the woman of my life . . .

She's quicker than me:

"Hi, everyone calls me Bella, but you can call me straight away."

I hesitate between laughing and running a mile. She doesn't give me time to choose:

"Sorry, I'm new, I saw that line on Twitter and found it funny. Now, writing it, I can see it's dumb. Is your name really Naruto, or is it a handle?"

"It's a manga character."

"I know . . . I'm going to drop the jokes."

I can't help smiling. I specialize in wisecracks that fall flat, my sense of humor is like some weirdo you watch out of the corner of your eye. I pull my hood back up and reply: "My name's Théo."

6
IRIS

I arrive exactly on time at Madame Beaulieu's. I open the door and announce myself in a loud voice, like the manager taught me to, on training day.

"Hello, it's Iris!"

Madame Beaulieu's voice greets me from the sitting room:

"Is that you, little tart?"

She's in a good mood.

As I do four mornings a week, I spend two hours with this lady, who has well and truly lost her marbles. I prepare her lunch, help her tidy her things, do a little cleaning, sometimes take her out for a stroll. Another care worker takes over from me in the afternoon, before her daughter returns in the evening. Madame Beaulieu doesn't differentiate between us, which is convenient: we all get the same nickname.

Next, I dash to the home of Monsieur Hamadi, who lost the use of his legs after being run over by a car, and then to Nadia's, a woman barely older than me, debilitated by multiple sclerosis.

"Must be a tiring job, no?" she asks me, while I'm ironing a dress.

"Can't complain."

"Must be difficult, all the same. Have you been doing it for long?"

I press the button, the iron spits out the steam, diluting her question. I don't know how to lie, I never have. If I reply with the truth, she'll try to find out more. Her ten-year-old son, lying on his front on the sofa, is reading. Perfect escape route.

"What are you reading?"

"*The Red and the Black*" he replies, without looking up. I pick up the sarcasm and decide to play his game:

"When you've finished that, I recommend Proust. It's easy reading, but you'll be well equipped for the day you tackle *Tintin*."

He cocks his head and looks me straight in the eye. In his eyes, I see both incredulity and disdain. He closes his book, gets up and leaves the sitting room. I get a glimpse of the book's cover: it is, indeed, the novel by Stendhal. His mother shrugs her shoulders:

"Thank goodness I saw him at birth, otherwise I'd think he'd been swapped with some other baby! At his age, I was reading Enid Blyton."

"At his age, I was brushing my Barbie's hair for her date with Ken."

She bursts out laughing, then hoists herself up onto her legs with the help of her sticks, and, in turn, leaves the room.

It's still warm outside when I leave Nadia's. She lives in the 17th arrondissement, I've nearly an hour's walk ahead to get to my rented studio. The pavements are packed, it's the time for heading home, with varying degrees of enthusiasm. Apparently, in France, ten million people live alone. I observe those around me and wonder which of them belong to that number. Do big strides betray an eagerness to be back with loved ones? Are those dragging their feet trying to delay the tête-à-tête with themselves? I've just spent six hours keeping isolated people company. How ironic. I stop for a few moments at a pedestrian crossing and, when the little man turns green, I continue on my way, dragging my feet.

7
JEANNE

Jeanne hadn't set foot in the second room for three months. It was the first time she'd gone that long without sewing. She opened the curtains, letting daylight back into the room. It was like returning to a familiar place after a long absence, she felt both at home and a stranger. She gazed at the sewing machine, the overlocker, the square of ecru viscose marked up with chalk, she ran a finger over the wooden worktable inherited from her mother, stroked the jumble of fabrics on the shelf, rolled a cotton reel in the palm of her hand. It was her den, her bunker. If, a few months ago, she'd been asked which room in the apartment she could never give up, she'd have answered without hesitation: the second room. And yet she'd made her decision.

She put on her raincoat and went out.

In her pocket, she could feel the squares of paper she'd written the notice on. She'd had to make an effort as, lately, her handwriting had become tighter and more uneven, as though tossed by a storm. Doubtless an effect of osteoarthritis, which worsened on rainy days. She used to moan about it a lot, before. It was a decline, an impediment, a sign of her body deteriorating. This had started with her sight, just before she hit forty-five. One morning, everything had been blurry when she'd woken up, having closed her eyes on her husband's face in clear focus. She had panicked, it had to be serious, sight didn't degenerate that quickly, but the ophthalmologist she'd urgently consulted had reassured her: it was common, at around her age, for visual acuity to diminish suddenly. Jeanne had found wearing glasses alienating: from now on, her body needed props to do what it had previously always done on its own. And from then on, this feeling had only got worse, what with the crowning of several teeth, the regulation of her cholesterol and blood pressure with drugs, the hip replacement, and the regular wearing of orthopedic supports to relieve the osteoarthritis. Ten years ago, the discovery of a tumor in her right breast had relegated her obsessions to the level of mere irritations. After her recovery, they had returned, slowly, insidiously, until they took up all their old space again. Much as she'd promised herself not to let them weigh her down anymore, she had welcomed them back: it was the sign that her life was back on track, back in its comfy slippers. No doubt she'd return to that state in a while, but for now, Jeanne was thinking about neither her osteoarthritis, nor her blood pressure. Her mind was entirely focused on the gaping void left by Pierre. Her every blood vessel, cell, millimeter of skin was primed to face grief's onslaught. Jeanne's entire being had been taken over by the absence.

The fruit-and-vegetable store owner, who counted Jeanne among his most loyal customers, was happy for her to put up a notice near the till. The tobacconist had a board for such notices, but warned her that it was rarely looked at. The grocer let her leave her piece of paper beside the counter, but the woman at the bakery wouldn't allow *her* counter to be cluttered up. Jeanne had never been one to insist, she thanked the woman, wished her a good day, and left the store. She was about to enter the hairdresser's next door when she felt a hand on her shoulder.

8
THÉO

Nathalie greets me warmly when I walk into the bakery at three minutes past seven: "Late again!"

I don't react. She's the one who was late the day niceness was handed out. The only thing more unpleasant than her is having a doctor's spatula stuck down your throat. If she knew why I'm late, she wouldn't give me a hard time for three measly minutes. Yesterday evening, when I got to Montreuil, my car wasn't there anymore. I'd listened to the cops, I'd parked it on another street, but I'd been careless, it was half on a pedestrian walkway. I called the pound, they confirmed that it was there and said I should go to the police station, where they'd give me a form to get the car back. So I did, but the police wanted me to pay a load of fines, for parking, for not getting the car inspected, for lack of insurance, for bald tires . . . they seem to think I'm the Bank of France. I said I'd go fetch my bank card, and then I beat it. I slept in the metro, for an hour or two, I'm not used to it anymore, and this morning I hurried to the pound to get my belongings back. I explained to the guy that my whole life was inside that car, but he wasn't interested. The result: I no longer own a thing apart from my phone, my wallet, and what I'm wearing.

I put on my work gear and join Philippe, who's training me, in the cold room. This morning, we're tackling the millefeuilles first. Philippe isn't the chatty type, he responds to questions with either grunts or gestures, but the moment we talk baking, he lights up and there's no stopping him anymore. He speaks of cakes as if they were living things—in fact, I once caught him whispering stuff to some. He explained to me that a cake made with respect and love always tastes better than the rest. He's a bit wacko, maybe that's why I like him.

Philippe knows that millefeuilles aren't my favorite thing, I always mess up the feathering, I just can't pipe in a straight line. It's like I'm over the limit. Try as I might, it's no good. It reminds me of my teacher in 3rd grade, who said I wrote like a pig, and made me miss recess to copy out letters. I even saw a psychomotor therapist every Wednesday, Laëtitia. She was cool, but I had to stop when I moved away. It's true that my handwriting's bad—even I can't always read what I've written—but it's no big deal, these days we rarely write by hand. Even at the apprenticeship center, we're allowed to use the computer.

Philippe watches while I pipe chocolate onto the icing. There's not a sound, when it comes to concentration, only tomato purée beats me.

"People are such a pain!"

Nathalie has just joined us in the lab. Neither Philippe nor I ask her for details, but she doesn't need us to. The cause of her annoyance: a lady who wanted to leave a notice on the counter.

"Is this a bakery or a bulletin board? I'm paid to sell bread, not to give information to tourists, or display leaflets. If she has a room to rent, she should just go to an agency, dammit! I've got better things to . . . "

I don't wait for her verbal diarrhea to end, I drop the piping bag and run for the exit. A lady has just walked past the glass door, I join her on the pavement and put my hand on her shoulder.

9
IRIS

It's almost four o'clock when my phone vibrates. I haven't set foot outside, just like every Saturday since living here. Apart from work and viewing apartments, my outings are confined to the grocery, the bakery, and the laundromat. Sprawled on the sofa-bed, I'm watching a documentary about an octopus and wondering exactly when my life became less exciting than a mollusk's. Getting this phone message is the high point of my day, up there with finding all those bits of strawberry in my lunchtime yogurt.

"Happy birthday, Iris! Thirty-three and all your own teeth!"

My mother doesn't trouble herself with niceties: every birthday message is a copy-and-paste of the preceding one, only the number changes. I'll reply with a "Thanks a lot, talk soon," just like I did to the sender of the single other message I've received today: my telecom provider. No one else has my new phone number.

While, on the screen, the octopus is about to become a mother, in my head, memories take over. Three years ago, on the evening of my thirtieth birthday, Jérémy came to pick me up outside work. I was surprised, he was supposed to be in London for two days, on a business trip. We'd been together for three months that seemed like forever. Right from the start, there had been this inevitability, as if our paths until then had come very close, with the sole aim of merging together. He blindfolded me and drove me in his car. When he took the blindfold off, I was at his place, facing all my loved ones shouting "Surprise!". My parents, my brother, my aunt, my cousins, my colleagues, and my gang of since-forever friends:

Marie, Gaëlle, and Mel. All the people who mattered, gathered together for me, by him. Everyone sang and danced, my mother gave me a bracelet that had belonged to her mother, and Jérémy's adoring looks followed my every move. I'd never been given a lovelier present.

The phone vibrates again, dragging me from my thoughts. My cheeks are wet—damned octopus dying as it gives birth. I expect to find another message from my mother, or some promo for a new tariff, but a notification tells me that the owner of my studio has written to me.

I've never met him. The rental is renewed weekly through an app, I pay online, and when I arrived, the keys were in a box with a security code. We rarely communicate, and only through the designated messaging account. According to his email address, he's called Gilles.

"Hi I need my studio back, you've paid to Sunday you can leave Monday have a nice day."

Puzzled, I reread the message several times. I'd made a point of checking with the owner that the studio was available medium term, he'd said yes, adding that it suited him, not having to start over every week with new tenants. I sit up to reply, suddenly nothing like a mollusk:

"Hello Gilles, I'm surprised, you told me I could stay here for a while. I'm close to finding accommodation, but still need a little time. Is that okay with you?"

He takes more than an hour to reply, during which I stare at the screen wondering if he's going to change his mind, or I'm going to end up on the streets. New message.

"Hi I need my studio back, you've paid to Sunday you can leave Monday have a nice day."

Same message, maybe he hasn't understood. I'm still hopeful:

"Thanks for your reply, but would it be possible to wait just a bit longer please? A month, let's say? I can pay you in full in advance."

This time, the response doesn't keep me waiting:

"Hi I need my studio back, you've paid to Sunday you can leave Monday have a nice day."

I try one last time, for the hell of it:

"Maybe you could allow me a week or two, so I can find alternative accommodation? I really do need it . . . "

I wait a few minutes, three little dots tell me he's writing a reply.

"Hi I need my studio back, you've paid to Sunday you can leave Monday have a nice day."

I remain frozen for a moment, letting it sink in that it's official: in two days' time, I won't have a roof over my head anymore. Then my thumbs, without checking first with my reason, type out my reply:

"O.K., have a nice day, Gilles the Pill."

I remain slumped for a few minutes, my brain needing all my energy to find a solution. I have nowhere to go. I know no one in Paris, except Mel, and I don't want her to know I'm here. Going back home isn't an option. I think again of my thirtieth birthday party. Never would I have imagined that, one day, I'd have no one and nowhere.

I get up, put on my jacket, my sneakers, and charge down the stairs. It's my birthday and, even without candles, I really fancy a cake.

10
JEANNE

The young man wore a black catering jacket and a mob-cap. He spoke fast, with a slight accent that Jeanne struggled to identify. Toulouse? Bayonne? She knew the south-west of France well, she and Pierre had often vacationed there. She preferred the Basque Country, with its verdant mountains, majestic coast, and unrivaled cheese. Jeanne raised her hand:

"Speak more slowly, my dear, I can't understand a single word."

"I heard you've got a room to rent, I'm looking for one, how much is it?"

Jeanne hadn't anticipated this situation. She'd written the notice with no real idea of what rent she'd ask, convinced that finding a lodger would take some time, if it happened at all. She had even found this thought reassuring. She reflected for a few seconds, and decided that the sum she was short of each month was reasonable:

"Two hundred euros."

"I'll take it!"

Jeanne took a good long look at the young man's face. He had gentle eyes, in contrast with his permanently knitted brows. She felt she could trust him, but Pierre had often warned her about her gullibility. The last time she'd opened her front door, she'd ended up with a ten-volume encyclopedia on her hands.

The door of the bakery opened with a tinkle. A young woman with brown hair came out, holding a little cake box. She walked a few steps before stopping to look for something in her bag.

"How old are you, young man?" asked Jeanne.

"Eighteen."

"You work here?"

"Yup, I'm an apprentice baker."

"I'll need some kind of guarantee. Could you put together your last three wage slips, along with a reference from your current landlord?"

He hesitated, before nodding. Jeanne took a notice out of her pocket and handed it to him:

"My number is on that, call me when you've got the documents."

The young man thanked her, seemed about to turn around, but then looked Jeanne straight in the eye:

"Madame, I really need an apartment. I don't even know where yours is, but I'm ready to cross Paris every day to get to work. I can't pay for a whole apartment, but a room would be awesome. I don't earn much, but I am conscientious. Please, give me a chance."

"Sorry to interrupt, but are you renting out a room?"

Jeanne and the young man turned their heads towards the voice asking the question. The young brunette who had just left the bakery was looking intently at Jeanne and smiling. She wore a denim jacket and her hair in a bob, and, under her green eyes, a little mascara had run.

"I am indeed," replied Jeanne. "I have an unused room in my apartment, and I'm looking for someone to lodge in it."

"And that someone is me!" the young man quickly added.

"That's not certain yet," Jeanne corrected.

"In which neighborhood is it?" the young woman asked.

Jeanne looked up and indicated a window on the third floor of a building some fifty meters away.

"Oh!" exclaimed the two young people in unison.

"*Madame*, I'm also interested in it," the young brunette continued. "Really interested. I need accommodation very soon. I'm on a decent salary, I'm discreet and reliable. You won't regret it."

Jeanne hesitated for a moment. The boy's face had clouded over while the girl's looked hopeful. Torn between her sense of justice and her empathy, she handed her a notice, too, and asked her to call her once she had put together her last three wage slips and a reference from her current landlord.

"I'll look closely at both of your documents," she assured them.

"I was here first, that stinks," the young man snapped.

The young woman shook her head:

"I'm sorry, I really need it."

"Forget it. I'm used to being screwed over."

He turned on his heel and dived back into the bakery. The young woman apologized again, and then also walked off. Jeanne returned to the fruit-and-vegetable store, the tobacconist's and the grocery, and took down her notices.

11
THÉO

I'm pissed off. I was ready to write a fake landlord's reference, I'm sure she'd have rented me her room, but then that bitch turned up. I stand no chance against a proper salary. I could see how the old woman was looking at me, she trusted me, I could have been okay at her place. And right next to work, as well. It was too good, it's never for me when it's good. In any case, I got annoyed and was rude, so it's over. And yet I've been warned often enough that I have too short a fuse, even saw a load of shrinks for it. One of them declared I was hyperactive, all the others just put it down to "the situation." They cracked me up, saying "the situation" instead of the actual words, as if their words would harm me even more than the facts.

The first shrink I saw, I must have been six or seven, he was called Dr. Leroux and made me do drawings while he played games on his phone. Then there was Dr. Volant, he was cool and really seemed to want to help me, but I didn't want to talk. I also remember Dr. Benjelloun, the most depressing guy in the universe. For the whole session, he kept repeating to me that the world was going wrong, humanity was done for, life was pointless since we'd all end up dead. I came out of there with all the optimism of a song by Adele. As an adolescent, I saw Dr. Merny for a few years. He'd smoke during consultations and his hair was always a mess. He amused me, even if I never knew what mood he'd be in: one session cheerful, the next grumpy. One time, he had his feet up on the desk when I entered his room.

"Know why I'm sitting like this?" he asked me.

"No."

"Because I've got a boil on my ass."

Another day, I phoned him to cancel an appointment at the last moment. I had a bad cold, I'd almost lost my voice, and he was in a foul mood. He told me that he wasn't at my disposal, that I should just call him when I was ready to respect my commitments. I don't know what came over me, but I started shouting, except all that came out was a ridiculous squeak. He listened to me telling him that I'd had enough of him talking to me that way, that I wasn't a piece of shit, that he should respect me, and then, very calmly, he explained to me that I could get back in touch when my voice no longer sounded like a dog's toy. He ended up retiring, otherwise I might have carried on seeing him. The last one I was sent to was Dr. Fabre, who would collect me from the waiting room, settle into his armchair, fix one eye on me, close the other eye, and then not move for the rest of the session. Not even an eyelash. I'd always prepare in advance what I'd tell him, otherwise it was total silence. Sometimes I'd pull a face at him or give him the finger, but he remained still as a statue. He only came back to life when the session was nearly over. I've never paid so much to watch someone sleeping.

My phone vibrates in the pocket of my jeans. I lock myself in the restroom, Philippe doesn't like me looking at my screen during work. It's Bella. We swapped numbers after our first conversation, and I deleted Tinder. She wanted us to swap photos, but I'd rather wait. She sent me one all the same, and it wasn't what I was expecting. She's a real looker, with long hair and a hot body. If she sees me, she'll vanish.

"Hey baby, missing you. I'm in English class, teacher sooo boring."

Whenever I read one of her messages, I get a weird feeling in my stomach. For a while now, I've been thinking of her several times a day. I promised myself not to fall in love anymore, it hurts too much having to pick yourself up again. Still, I must tell her I don't like that pet name. My mother called me that. I send a quick reply, kinda half-detached, half-concerned, and, as I put my phone away, I feel the folded room ad deep in my pocket. I take the plunge, before Philippe comes to find me and I chicken out.

"Madame, I'm so sorry I lost my temper earlier on. Despite appearances, I'm not a bad guy. I promise I'll pay each month and won't disturb you. I'll listen to my music with headphones and smoke outdoors. I could bake you cakes, I'm pretty good at it. Having said that, I don't want to lie to you—I can't give you my current landlord's reference because my current landlord is the metro. Regards, Théo Rouvier."

12
Iris

My whole life fits into one suitcase. It's Jérémy who gave it to me, one Friday night in December. It was shortly after my birthday party, we'd just learnt about my father's illness and were all in shock. Jérémy came to wait for me outside work. I felt like doing just one thing: collapsing on my sofa with a packet of chips and a TV series requiring only the superficial part of my brain. But seeing him swept away all tiredness. He lived in La Rochelle, I lived in Bordeaux, we got together whenever we could, and the rest of the time, missed each other. He didn't drive me home, he took the bypass and ignored my many attempts at finding out where we were going. Before him, I'd been in a long relationship with a man who, when it came to surprises, was about the level of a Kinder egg, so I let myself be led with genuine pleasure.

"But I haven't got my things!" I protested as we arrived at the airport.

Out of the car's trunk, he pulled a green suitcase, bought for the occasion:

"I've packed it, nothing's missing."

We had a dreamy weekend, a magical break, in Venice. For two days, I forgot the hospital corridors and the look in my father's eyes. We walked, ate, made love, ate, took photos, ate, visited places, ate, laughed, ate, made love, ate, talked, ate.

During the return flight, while I was gripping his fingers, he handed me a small box. Inside, a key.

"I'd like you to move in with me," he murmured.

It got me hard, right there, in the chest. I already loved him so much.

I left Bordeaux six months later. I wanted to stay close to my father until the very end.

I stop on the third floor to get my breath back. The elevator in Nadia's building isn't working, on the very day I'm lugging a suitcase heavier than me. My aim is to reach the eighth floor before I've developed Vin Diesel's muscles.

On the fourth, I'm overtaken by a gentleman of about twice my age who hops from step to step like Super Mario and greets me without the slightest sign of breathlessness.

On the fifth, I come very close to abandoning my suitcase.

On the sixth, I come very close to abandoning my lungs.

On the seventh, I pray. My lungs who art on fire, forgive me my cigarettes, as we forgive those who don't inhale, lead us not into temptation, but deliver us from Marlboros. Amen.

On the eighth, when I open the door to Nadia's apartment, I'm breathing like a punctured tire, but I put on the smile of one who has conquered Kilimanjaro.

She's in the kitchen, preparing a tajine. The aroma of the sauce, with its prunes and almonds, instantly reminds me of my friend Gaëlle, who liked to cook this dish. I banish the memory before nostalgia gets the better of me.

"Coming to live here?" Nadia asks, clocking my suitcase.

"Of course, didn't I tell you?"

She laughs, before slumping back into her wheelchair.

"It's an off day," she tells me. "My legs won't carry me for more than a few minutes."

"It'll be better tomorrow."

As I say it, I realize how inane it sounds. Supportive sayings are often like that, useful only to mask one's powerlessness. I never heard the expression "that's life" as often as when I was confronted with death.

"Seriously," Nadia insists, "why do you have a suitcase?"

Blood rushes to my cheeks and I start to giggle stupidly, like I do whenever I lie. Escaping towards the cleaning-products cupboard, I spout the answer I'd prepared, like a poem learnt by heart and recited to the whole 3rd-grade class. A story about some clothes I need to return to a friend, and whose place I'm going to straight from work.

I would have preferred it to be true. As I walk back down the eight floors, after two hours with Nadia, I still have no idea where I'm going to sleep.

On the fourth floor, I pause to check my messages on the rentals app. I've sent a dozen requests to landlords, not one has replied.

On the third, I stop to look for other apartments and send some new requests. Super Mario runs down the stairs.

On the second, I look at the price of hotels, check my bank account, and allow myself one floor to come to a decision.

On the first, I find a hotel that's decently priced, but the reviews bemoan a shocking lack of cleanliness and comfort. "The only star this place deserves is for being shit," states one. In my situation, I can't be fussy, I book a room.

On the ground floor, I send a text message.

"Hello madame, I just wanted to confirm my interest in your room for rent. And please know that, if it weren't for my tricky situation, I'd never have interrupted your conversation with the young man, who also seems in real need of a home. If you've not yet made your choice, I'd understand if you favor him. Regards, Iris."

October

13
JEANNE

Jeanne arrived at the cemetery at the same time as every other day. It was an appointment she was determined not to be late for. That morning she had been to the hairdresser's to get her ends trimmed. She had long hair that she gathered into a chignon to go out. Once every season, when the moon was waxing, she would have a few centimeters cut off to keep her hair strong.

Mireille, who had done her hair for over twenty years, had asked her how Pierre was, concerned that she hadn't seen him for ages. Like every time this question stabbed her in the heart, Jeanne hadn't managed to say that he was dead. "I've lost him," she had said, because that was exactly how she felt.

The bench close to Pierre's grave was occupied. A woman was sitting on it, back straight, eyes staring into space. Jeanne got no response to her greeting, but took no offence: Pierre awaited her. She laid her hand on his photo, stroked it, then leant towards his ear to whisper:

"I look for you everywhere, my love. In the rumpled sheets, in the steam of the shower, in the mirror, in the curtain that moves, I look for you in Boudine's eyes, in the sound of steps on the stairs, in your shirts on their hangers. I look for you in my memories, in a TV program, in a song, in a voice that resonates, I look for you in a gust of wind, a flash of lightning, the searing heat of the sun. I look for you in your bottle of cologne, in your half-used tube of toothpaste, in your unfinished shopping list, in your phone's answering machine, in the video of our last vacation, in the photos I never sorted out. I look for you on street corners, on pedestrian walkways, and in parks, in the shade of trees, on the terraces of cafés, in the line at the grocery store, I look for you when the phone rings, when there's a knock at the door, when I open the mailbox. I look for you at three minutes past midnight, at seven thirty-four, at noon, at seventeen past five, at six past nine. I look for you behind my back, in my neck, beneath my hands, against my belly. I look for you everywhere and I don't find you. I have lost you, my love."

She wiped her cheeks and turned to the bench. The woman had disappeared. Jeanne removed the dead leaves from the plants, watered those that needed it, wiped the plaques, and finally sat down.

"I promised you I'd find a solution for the apartment. I've kept my word. I'm not sure you'd approve of the idea, but I've given it a lot of thought and I have no choice. I'm going to rent out the second room. I don't sew anymore, don't feel like it anymore. I've stored all the gear in the cellar and Victor helped me put a bed and chest of drawers in the room. The lodger is called Iris, she's a care worker, and seems reliable to me. She arrives this evening."

Jeanne went quiet for a moment, her eyes fixed on the photo of her husband. He didn't respond, she continued:

"I'm not totally at ease with it, I've never shared my life with anyone but you. Victor told me it would be a good thing to do, that I'd feel less lonely. I don't feel lonely, I feel without you."

She stopped again, this time to hold back the tears threatening to well up. She kept the rest of her concerns to herself, and moved on to the gossip she had gleaned from Mireille. Pierre had always relished it as much as she did. It had become a ritual, he never came home from the hairdresser's—which he went to more often than Jeanne—without an update on the local tittle-tattle. Madame Minot's new lover, the scandal concerning Monsieur Schmidt, or the latest escapades of the Liron children would make them laugh like naughty kids themselves.

The sky had darkened when Jeanne left her husband, saying see you tomorrow. She wound her scarf around her neck, attached Boudine's leash, and headed for the exit, her shoulders more hunched than usual. It weighed heavy on her, the guilt of not having told him the whole truth.

Another letter awaited her in the mailbox. She hurried up to her apartment and opened the envelope before even taking off her raincoat.

Spring 1993

After seeing Ghost *at the cinema, Jeanne goes to the hairdresser's to get the same short cut as Demi Moore. She'd hesitated for several weeks and then finally decided, telling herself that hair did grow back again. She hasn't spoken to Pierre about it, she wants to surprise him. He's always known her with her long brown hair. Jeanne rarely goes to the hairdresser's, she doesn't have a particular one. She randomly picks a salon and lands on a hairdresser who confirms that the Demi Moore style is all the rage right now, and that she's used to doing it. On her way home, Jeanne feels good. Light as a bird. She feels like Demi Moore. Pierre is there when she arrives. She feels like an adolescent, torn between impatience for and apprehension of those first times. He's surprised. He stares at her, asks her to turn around, switches on the light to see her better. He finally tells her that she looks wonderful, that the cut sets off her well-defined jaw and straight nose. "Know who you remind me of?" he asks. Jeanne is thrilled. She knows he's going to compare her to Demi Moore, doesn't doubt it, but she plays the game and shakes her head. He smiles tenderly, the smile of someone who's paying a marvelous compliment, and says: "Mireille Mathieu."*

Jeanne had forgotten this anecdote. She surprised herself by laughing as she thought back to it, before realizing that she'd better sit down. Her legs were about to give way. The emotion was just as intense as for the first letter, maybe even more intense. She had hoped for this second letter as much as she had dreaded it. There was no indication of its sender, but for now, that wasn't the most important thing. For a few seconds, Jeanne had been immersed in the world that no longer existed.

14
Théo

I can't get over it. When the old woman called me to say it was okay for the room, I thought she'd dialed the wrong number. The last time I was lucky was at a bingo game organized by the hunters' association, a couple of years ago, at least. I was hanging out with Manon, Ahmed, and Gérard (who isn't as old as his name suggests), and we went past the village hall, saw all those people studying cards with numbers on them as if searching for Waldo, and we fancied a go. We took just one card for the four of us—it cost an arm and a leg. It was the very last round, the biggest prize. We were missing just one more number to have a full house: the 63. Beside us, a woman who had left home without her eyebrows was waiting for the 31. She had a dozen cards and even some magnetic counters, which she gathered up with a magnetic wand. We had only chickpeas, but that didn't stop us from winning. When the 63 was called, we jumped for joy as if we'd won the World Cup, running around, hugging everyone, but we soon calmed down when we discovered what we'd won. The look on everyone's face when we returned to the home with an actual pig, I cry with laughter whenever I think of it. The pig became our mascot, we called him Bordeau Chesnel, after the potted-pork brand. I think of him sometimes, when I go down memory lane, but then stop myself, because my mother always said that crying is for the weak.

I ring on the entry phone, the door opens. There are mailboxes and a small courtyard with some plants and garbage cans. I'm not sure where to go, a guy sticks his head out of a ground-floor window and asks if he can help. I don't even know the name of the lady with the room.

"I'm here to see a lady with a bun."

He slams the window shut and, seconds later, comes out of a red door holding a cat. So quick, it's like he's been beamed down. He tells me he's Victor Giuliano, the caretaker of the building. He seems to know I was coming.

"Madame Perrin lives on the third, the stairs are over here."

He shows me the way, I thank him and get going, but he catches hold of my arm.

"She's a nice lady, you know."

"O.K."

He doesn't let go of me:

"No harm must come to her."

"Oh? You mean I can't smother her while she sleeps and gobble up her brain? Too bad."

Victor drops my arm and steps back. I feel obliged to stress that I'm joking, that I've never liked the taste of brains. He laughs nervously, assuring me that he knew that. I pretend to believe him, despite his expression being that of a turkey coming across a butcher on Christmas Eve.

The old lady opens the door just as I reach the third floor. She asks me to wait on the doormat and then places two large rectangles of fabric in front of my feet:

"Now you can come in."

I step over the rectangles and find myself in a small entrance hall. She stops me from going any further:

"Put on the skates, please!"

"The what?"

She points at the two pieces of cloth and explains that they are indoor "skates," to protect the parquet floor.

"Either you keep your shoes on and slide on the pads, or you take your shoes off. It's the original parquet, I take good care of it, but it's easily damaged. You don't have a bag?"

I shake my head and put my feet on her thingies, then follow her to my new room, sliding one foot and then the other. You can call me Torvill & Dean.

The room is small and pretty dark, but it'll do. There's a single bed, a chest of drawers, a desk and a white rug, seemingly made of Santa's pubes. I skate over to the window looking out onto the courtyard.

"I'll leave you to settle in," she tells me, closing the door. "I'll show you around the rest later."

Finally alone. I kick off my sneakers and fall back onto the bed. I can't stop smiling, I must look daft, but if I don't smile today, when will I? I have a home. I have a home. I can't believe it. If I had more space, I'd do a triple lutz. I was sure that woman outside the bakery had trumped me. She must be pissed off, but it's just karma. She tried to push in front of me, had no pity for me, I won't have any for her.

I grab my phone to tell my pals the news, but change my mind at the last moment. I've not been in touch with them since leaving, I'm not going to shove it in their faces when they're still stuck there. I'd rather send a message to Bella, I've not heard from her since yesterday. We usually write all the time, whenever we can. In the evening, it can go on for hours when she's got nothing to do. She looks after her sick father, on top of her history-of-art studies and waitressing job. We have loads in common. She confided stuff to me that she'd never spoken about before, so I started telling her my secrets, too. I get the feeling she really understands me. Yesterday, I sent her a photo of myself. She'd been on about it for a while. I didn't feel great once I'd sent it, I was scared she'd find me ugly. But she said "I love you." That did something weird to my heart. I've not been told that often. Never knew you could grow attached to someone you've never seen.

"Hi Bella, all O.K.? Guess where I'm writing to you from <3"

Just as I'm sending the message, I hear the doorbell ring in the apartment. A few minutes later, two voices. I open the door and stick my head out. A woman is just stepping onto some cloth skates. When she looks up, I recognize her: the woman from outside the bakery, followed by a green suitcase.

15
Iris

I hadn't used cloth skates since I was a kid. My grandmother made us use them when she'd just cleaned the floor. My cousin and I would play at who could skate furthest. He was two years older than me and very cocky. My competitive spirit was surfacing, so I'd do my utmost not to let him win. So much so that I ended up kissing the corner of the wall, found myself with a split lip, and then sticky tape to close it up, and was deprived of kids TV as punishment for getting blood on the freshly polished parquet.

Just as I look up, my eyes meet those of the young guy from the bakery. I smile at him, he shuts the door.

"I decided to take both of you, I have two spare rooms. Come, I'll show you yours. By the way, my name is Jeanne."

I follow her to the end of the corridor. The room isn't very big, but it has everything I need, including a plump comforter I already feel like snuggling under. Jeanne leaves me, suggesting I come and find her in ten minutes to discuss sharing arrangements. Two minutes is all I need to empty my suitcase. It contains only my desperation to leave, just enough clothes to last a few days. I couldn't see any further. I'm dreaming of a hot shower—at the hotel I stayed five nights in, there was just a trickle of tepid water. I take in the white curtains, clearly handmade, and the wallpaper covered in clouds, wondering whether I'll ever manage, one day, to feel really at home. It's the first time, since leaving La Rochelle, that I'm really settling. I took the "one step at a time" approach, feeling my way along, without knowing what tomorrow would bring. Having a place of my own is reassuring, even if I'll obviously have to leave it in the medium term.

The moment I open the door to what seems to be the sitting room, I'm violently attacked by a ferocious animal. I run to the first place of safety in sight, and find myself perched on a green-velvet sofa, before the baffled gazes of Jeanne and the boy.

"Don't be afraid, my dear, Boudine just wants to welcome you."

"I didn't know you had a guard dog."

The boy sniggers:

"Never seen such a massive pit bull."

"Boudine isn't a pit bull!" Jeanne cries, taking her dog into her arms. "She's a miniature dachshund. Come now, my darling, don't listen to a word they're saying."

My dog phobia began the day when—I must have been seven—the apricot-colored poodle belonging to the neighbor came into our garden and mistook my calf for roast chicken. I tried to free myself, swung my leg in all directions, but it was no good, the dog was flying like a flag but wouldn't let go. I screamed, my father showed up and managed to remove the assailant. I came out of it with a few stitches and a terror of all canines, whatever their size. I underwent therapy when Jérémy said he wanted to adopt a Labrador, but it didn't work. A disappointment for him, as he often reminded me.

With shaky legs, I step back down onto the floor and join my new roommates around a wooden table. The boy points at the green sofa:

"You've lost something."

I scan the sofa, nothing. I stand up, take a closer look, slide my hands between the cushions, still nothing.

"I can't see a thing. What did I lose?"

"Your dignity," he replies, solemnly.

Sharing this apartment is off to a most auspicious start.

16
Jeanne

Since Pierre's death, Jeanne had got into the habit of going to bed early. She had tried to maintain her daily routine as far as possible, but certain habits no longer made any sense. With him, she would watch a movie to the end, then they would chat about it, exchange impressions, and sometimes, thanks to a familiar scene, wander down memory lane. She no longer watched movies to the end. She found she couldn't be gripped anymore, either by a screen or a book. Her mind remained on the surface, floating in another fiction, where Pierre had the leading role.

On that evening, when the lodgers arrived, Jeanne had gone to bed even earlier than usual. She had a strange feeling she couldn't shake, and had hoped to sleep it off. For several weeks, she had seen sleep as a refuge. When it didn't come naturally, she would help it along with sleeping pills prescribed by the doctor. It was the only way she had found to silence her noisy grief, to put it on pause and catch her breath, ready to face reality's next big wave.

She wasn't in her own home anymore. That's what she'd been thinking all evening. There were strangers at her table—charming as they might be—and her apartment, and thus all that it represented, was transformed. She had made the decision quickly, driven by the fear of not being able to pay her bills, without considering the consequences. It had happened before she'd even had time to think that it really would happen. These people were going to drink from the same glasses as Pierre, lay their heads on the same pillowcases, their hands on the same door handles. Already, the girl had even stood on the sofa, exactly where he would sit.

Jeanne reached out to stroke Boudine, who had taken Pierre's place in the bed. The dog wagged its tail. She couldn't go back now. They had drawn up a lease. The boy had thanked her a dozen times, and she had seen Iris holding back tears when signing the document. They had then worked out a semblance of rules, so they could all live together harmoniously. It was a first for the three of them, each had made suggestions, and they had voted on them. In that way it was agreed that visitors weren't welcome, that the housework would be done on a yet-to-be-decided rota, that any rooms used would be tidied and cleaned by each user, that noise was banned, that the bedrooms were private places to which no one but their occupant had the right to enter, that a shelf in the fridge and the cupboard would be allocated to each of them, that meals didn't have to be shared, that the rent would be paid on the 5th of the month, and that everyone's sleep should be respected. The rules would evolve as the apartment share progressed, but the foundations were laid.

At the end of the meeting, Jeanne had suggested that they have supper together. Théo had declined, saying he'd had a sandwich before leaving the bakery. Iris had accepted, and they had shared the squash soup and quiche Lorraine that Jeanne had prepared, presuming they wouldn't have had time to do any shopping. They had chatted about this and that, and then Iris had cleared the table and, in turn, retired to her room, but not without first making a particular request to Jeanne: "I'd rather my name wasn't on the entry phone." Although surprised, Jeanne had agreed.

Finally, she sank into a dreamless sleep. At three in the morning, woken by a sound, she got up, put on her slippers and dressing gown, and gently opened the door onto the corridor. The sound got louder. Jeanne moved towards it, trying to avoid the squeaky floorboards, then put her ear to the door of the third room. The sound was very clear now and left no doubt as to its source: Iris was sobbing.

17
Théo

I arrived early at work. Nathalie's eyes popped so far out of her head, I saw her brain. It took me exactly four minutes to get there from home.

Home. I hadn't said that for a long time. The first time I wound up at the children's home, I was five years old. I don't remember much, except clenching my fists so hard that my fingernails cut into my palms, and my mother's howls when they took me away. I also remember that kick from Jason, an older boy who hadn't appreciated my not responding when he'd said hello. And my little backpack with a koala bear head.

Yesterday, I signed my first lease. I felt grown-up. One day, I'll have an apartment all to myself. I don't have many dreams, they make a god-awful mess when they shatter. But that one I really believe in. I want to turn the key in *my* lock, open *my* fridge door, lie on *my* sofa, play *my* music, and enjoy *my* life. If I pass my vocational certificate, I'd like to work in a large restaurant or a tearoom. Somewhere people eat, to see their faces as they taste my cakes. That's what I like best, cooking for someone. The moment it makes them happy.

I join Philippe in the cold room. He's not alone. He introduces Leïla to me. She's going to help Nathalie at the counter. I knew nothing about it, but it's like that here, they don't give a toss about communicating, it's all balls to them. Philippe sends me to fill the dessert glasses, and stays with the new girl. My phone keeps vibrating. I end up locking myself in the restroom. It's Bella.

"Théo, I need you."

"Théo pls it's urgent!"

"I'm in the shit!!!"

I'm so concerned, I phone her. It's the first time I'll hear her voice. Just as my call's going through, I get a new message:

"I can't answer, I'm at the hospital."

I cut the call and message instead to ask her what's going on.

"He's had a heart attack, he's in a coma. I'm scared . . . "

Bella often talks to me about her father. Her mother died two years ago, she only has him now. She's told me several times that she'd never get over it, if she lost him.

"I need you Théo."

"Do you want me to come?"

Someone knocks on the door. I know it's Philippe. I should come out, but Bella replies to me:

"No, not now. My debit card got pinched this morning and they're asking for a two-hundred euro deposit to operate on my father. Could you send me a PCS voucher?"

My stomach lurches. I ask her what a PCS voucher is, but I already know the answer.

"You need to go to a tobacconist's, you ask for a two-hundred euro voucher, they'll give you a code number, and then you just give it to me."

"O.K., Bella. I'll deal with it right away."

Phillippe knocks on the door, harder. I need several minutes to stop shaking. Don't know how I fell for it. And yet I've heard loads of stories of people being scammed on dating sites. I'm really dumb. Just throw me a few crumbs of affection, chuck in an "I love you," and my brain stops working. It's my weak point, I go soft on contact with love. I'm the opposite of a dick, I suppose. That's why Manon dumped me: she found me too nice. When she first met me, I was a big mouth and loved fighting, that's what she liked. So, as soon as I started writing slam poems to her, picking bunches of flowers for her, and trying to talk it over when she was nasty to me, she didn't like it, and she cleared off with a piece of my heart.

There's hammering on the door. I come out, Philippe is waiting for me there, arms crossed:

"Shame you don't shit petroleum, you'd be a millionaire."

Leïla covers her mouth so as not to giggle, and Nathalie's burst of laughter can be heard from the store. I walk past them without a word and return to my countertop. They can all fuck off.

18
Iris

"Is that you, little tart?"

"Yes, yes, it's me!"

Madame Beaulieu is pleased to see me. Every day now, since she told me she loves Scrabble, we play it together. Owing to her cognitive difficulties, the rules have been simplified: we can place any word we want wherever we want. She sometimes asks me the meaning of a word, and I do my best to come up with one. So, it turns out that the "ptiwob" is an orange tropical flower, that one might "muqir" in public when hot, and that the young of the zebra are "zubs."

She watches me as I do the housework. At first, I took this to be supervision, but then understood that, actually, she sees me as a kind of show. I'm a ballerina with a feather duster. She's obsessively anxious about her underwear. Every three minutes, she frets over whether she has enough underpants. I reassure her: they're kept in the closet, on the third shelf. She nods, reassured, then starts again three minutes later. Her daughter, on the rare occasions I've come across her, has told me about the active, strong mother the disease had stolen from her. "She marched for women's rights, she dared to get divorced, she built up her business and managed thirty-odd people. She was a great lady. I can't accept seeing her reduced to this."

Occasionally, a flash of lucidity breaks through Madame Beaulieu's hazy sky. Like today, when she looks me straight in the eye when I place "govhnoox" on triple word score.

"Do you like your job?"

I nod and am about to change the subject when, remembering that she'll instantly forget, I decide to open up:

"Care work isn't my real job."

"Really? What is your real job?"

I haven't spoken about it for a long time, I'm no longer even sure that my old life existed.

"I'm a physio. I worked in a practice with another physiotherapist and an osteopath."

Madame Beaulieu frowns:

"But why the devil aren't you practicing anymore?"

"I couldn't stay there, I had to find a job fast. I knew that, with care work, companies are often looking for staff. And also . . ."

I break off, for fear of going too far, but Madame Beaulieu's curiosity won't let me:

"Yes?"

"It was too risky to keep doing the same job."

She stares at me for a long time. I regret having spoken, fear she wants to know more. I've buried the truth so deep, it's become painful to exhume it. The change is subtle, but still visible. Madame Beaulieu's gaze loses intensity, starts to waver, as though looking through me. It's no longer me she's staring at, it's her other world. After several minutes, she ends up asking me what "govhnoox" means.

My day finishes early, the apartment is empty when I get home. After living here for a week, I've gotten to know the others' routines: Jeanne is never home before six, and Théo arrives around an hour later. The pit bull isn't here either, which I can't say I'm sorry about.

I fill up the kettle and light the stove. I open two cupboards before finding the tea. The kitchen has remained stuck in the nineties, with its pine and blue handles. Everything on view is neat and tidy, but that can't be said of the rest. Inside the drawers, it's a war zone. The cutlery is thrown in any old how, loose pasta and grains of rice lie around empty boxes, and I found a packet of flour that was older than me. "It's my organized chaos," Jeanne said, defensively, noticing my astonishment. I didn't admit that I was just like her, fearing she'd want to replace me with some domestic goddess. If she knew. I'm paid to organize, clean, tidy for others, when I'm incapable of doing so for myself. I'm a flipflop-wearing cobbler, a vegan butcher, a bald barber. Jérémy was my complete opposite, he would store his things in boxes that were labeled and sorted in alphabetical order.

I've just poured hot water into a William and Kate cup when my phone rings.

"Everything okay, darling?"

"Hi Mom."

"Everything okay?" she insists.

Her voice betrays her concern. She knows. I don't get a chance to reply.

"Iris, Jérémy's mother phoned me. She says you disappeared two months ago. Is that because of the wedding?"

19
JEANNE

Jeanne entered the building wondering if it was a good idea. She had always wanted to believe in the existence of another world, another life, unlike Pierre, who was a paid-up Cartesian. So, when the man had phoned her, she'd seen it as a sign.

On the black door, a gilt plate was to the point:

Bruno Kafka
The voice of absent ones

The hall had been turned into a waiting room. Jeanne walked across the patchwork of rugs and sat down in a well-worn leather armchair.

As a child, a neighbor's story had left an impression on her. He told anyone who would listen that he and his wife had promised each other that the first to die would contact the surviving spouse, one way or another. On the evening after his wife's funeral, he had clearly felt her presence in the bedroom. He had tapped three times on the wall and waited. A few seconds later, he'd heard three taps in reply. That was enough for little Jeanne, who was already asking herself many questions about the meaning and ending of life, to cling firmly to the idea that something awaited humans on the other side.

Over the years, doubt had crept in, despite several painful bereavements that could have done with some certainties. Nevertheless, she kept her hopes alive by reading the testimonies of people who had communicated with a deceased loved one, or had a near-death experience.

Maybe this Monsieur Kafka would be the alchemist who could turn hope into conviction.

The door opened and a man, small and bald, welcomed her with a smile:

"Madame Perrin? I was expecting you."

Jeanne stood up, trying to stop shaking. She was wearing the red blouse Pierre was so fond of.

She moved into a darkened room. The shutters were closed and the only light came from candles, dotted here and there. Monsieur Kafka invited her to sit on a divan and sat opposite her, on the other side of a round table.

"Madame Perrin, I contacted you because I have a message for you. Your husband was called Pierre, wasn't he?"

Jeanne silently nodded, her throat being too tight to utter a sound. The man opened a note pad, picked up a pen, and continued:

"Pierre wishes to reassure you: he is at peace, serene."

Jeanne felt tears welling up. She managed to articulate a question:

"Can you see him?"

"Absolutely. He's beside you, standing. Can you feel his hand on your shoulder?"

Jeanne concentrated, but felt nothing.

"Yes," she replied.

"He's speaking to me of your children. I can't quite make out how many. Two, is that right?"

"We didn't have any children."

The man seems put out:

"A pet perhaps? A cat?"

"A dog."

"Absolutely! That's it! Communication can be a little fuzzy, but it is indeed a dog. Pierre is happy knowing you're together. He asks you not to worry, he'll be there when you join him on the other side. I sense that he's very serene."

The medium breaks off for a moment, then takes the cap off his pen:

"Do you have any questions for him? I'm here to transcribe his answers. As I told you on the phone, my five senses are at the service of the deceased."

Jeanne had the answer to her main question: one day she would be back with her Pierre. She did, however, have one question for the medium:

"How did you get my phone number? No one ever calls me on the landline."

"Your husband gave it to me, when he revealed himself to me. I contacted you at his request. Any other questions?"

"I just want to know if he's well."

"Then you can sleep easy: he's in great form. For someone dead, I mean. Forgive me," he said, bursting out laughing, "I have a medium's sense of humor!"

Jeanne stayed a little longer, then paid the two hundred euros the séance cost, in cash as requested. She stood up, not knowing whether she was convinced or not. The man accompanied her to the door and, before letting her go, whispered a parting shot:

"Pierre thanks you for the red blouse."

20
THÉO

It's my first karate lesson. I found a second-hand kimono and took the metro to Montreuil after work. This morning I left a note in the kitchen to let Jeanne know I'd be home a bit later. Don't know why I did that, she's not that fussed about us, thank God, I'd worried she'd be a control freak. But the other evening, I got back half an hour later than usual and found her pressed up to the spyhole on the door. I got the impression she was concerned, but maybe I was just seeing things.

There's about twenty of us in the dojo, oldies, kids, women and men. The instructor is a guy in his forties, with a physique that's no great shakes, but a look in his eye you wouldn't want to mess with. He doesn't speak loudly, but stresses every consonant. It's like he's speaking German, but in French. I slotted myself between a little boy and a woman with red hair. The warm-up lasts a good twenty minutes and reduces my life expectancy by at least ten years. I feel like I'm at a boot camp, we run, we crawl, we jump, we do push-ups, I sweat. Next we have to reproduce movements called kihon, then sequences called kata. At first sight, it looks easy, but in reality, it deserves to be called a martial art. I have four limbs that have decided to tell my brain to go hang. My body was delivered before my coordination had been fine-tuned. I'm perfectly able to do a movement with my left arm, and, potentially, do the same movement simultaneously with my right arm. But if I'm asked to do two different movements, or worse, add the legs, I'm stuck. System error. I once tried to play the guitar, and the guitar has never forgotten it. The boy beside me gives me advice. He wears a green belt and is super precise. Makes you want to keep at it.

Because of the children's home and the many moves, I never got to do a sport properly. I played football with friends, but didn't really enjoy it, it was just something to do. At school, I loved handball but never got to play it in a club.

There are a few minutes left, the instructor asks us to pick a partner and practice combat skills. Naturally, I turn to the boy with the green belt. He accepts. He's called Sam and is ten years old. When I try to make contact with him, he makes fun of me, which I'm not thrilled about, but I choose to keep shtum out of consideration for my nasal septum. And anyhow, he's not wrong: every time I throw a kick, I lose my balance, like Van Damme on a windy day.

When I get home I'm feeling blue. It hits me sometimes, just like that, without warning. It means everything's fine. When it's not fine, you have to fight, there's no room for my mood to express itself. Maybe it's because of that woman I came across earlier, on the banks of the river. She was laughing loudly, dancing, seemed happy, as if she'd just had good news. And then suddenly she was reeling, tried to steady herself on thin air, and she fell. Flat on her back, she was crying and laughing at the same time. She was dead drunk. A spectacle I'm only too familiar with.

Jeanne and Iris are watching TV. Jeanne is on the sofa, Iris on a chair. They greet me, I dash into the kitchen. I'm famished, must have burnt a million calories during that training. The note I left for Jeanne is still on the worktop. She's written something underneath.

"There's a roast-chicken leg and carrots in the fridge, you just need to warm them up."

My shelf is almost empty, just a slice of ham and some Gruyère left. I often have a sandwich at the bakery. I put the dish in the microwave, pour myself a glass of cola, and, without thinking, go to sit down with my two roomies.

21
Iris

The emergency-department waiting room is packed. I've been waiting my turn for almost an hour, and it's not about to come. My case isn't considered a priority, I'm not wounded or in pain. And yet I came pretty close to knocking on heaven's door.

It's all the fault of Victor, the caretaker, who got it into his head to clean the stairs until they were as bright as his ideas. At seven in the morning, exactly when everyone uses them (the stairs, not Victor's ideas.)

I left home at the same time as Théo, who is always as pleasant as a pap smear. From the very top step, I sensed I wasn't going to reach the ground floor in a vertical position. My foot slipped without asking my permission, the rest of my body didn't have time to register the information, it fell limply. It was like one of those push puppets that collapse when you press the button. Or a cheese soufflé taken too soon out of the oven, but I admit a clear preference for the first image. I tried to grab hold of Théo, but only succeeded in grabbing hold of his sleeve, which just dropped me like some tiresome ex. I then tumbled down a dozen steps on my bottom and back, in almost filmic slow motion, giving me time to get to know every bone, muscle, and tendon in my body. I formed a particularly deep bond with my coccyx. When I finally came to a stop, I found myself, by my dazed reckoning, in a position usually only seen in contortionist shows (or Picasso's paintings). I thought I heard my roommate laughing, but maybe it was my perineum crying.

Théo helped me up:

"Are you okay? Nothing broken?"

After checking, I could affirm that each limb seemed to be in its originally allotted place. I clung to the arm he offered me, not letting go until the ground floor, where he asked me for the second time if I wanted him to call an ambulance.

"I'll be okay," I assured him.

As soon as he'd disappeared from my field of vision, I called the agency that employs me to alert them to my absence, then took myself to the emergency department. I had to check that everything was *really* okay.

On the beige plastic seats facing me, a couple are tapping away on a mobile phone, reawakening a dormant memory. One evening, Jérémy found me playing on mine. The aim of the game: forming words of varying lengths with letters taken from a pile. I was a seasoned player, having discovered letter games as a child, when my parents gave me Speak & Spell and Boggle. Later, I'd spent hours solving endless crossword puzzles. Jérémy asked if he could play with me. I gladly accepted, happy to share my passion and, I admit, dazzle him with my prowess. I kept finding winning letter combinations and increasing my score, while he struggled to find a few words. Realizing this, I forced myself to slow down so he could join in, but as soon as a word came to me, I couldn't help writing it on the screen. Before we'd reached the end of that level, Jérémy stood up without a word. I instantly realized he was upset. I joined him in the bedroom, where he was lying on the bed. I jumped beside him, imitating the cat, to cheer him up. I insisted he come back to the game, promised I'd give him time to join in. Faced with his silence, I even apologized to him. He didn't move, his eyes closed, his face expressionless. He didn't speak to me for two days. I felt I'd been conceited, childish and nasty. One evening, he came home from work like his old self, as if those two days hadn't happened. He never spoke about it. A while later, when I wanted to play on my phone, the app had disappeared.

"Madame Iris Duhin?"

I get up and follow the intern into the cubicle. She asks me to get undressed, lie on the examining couch, and explain why I've come. I describe my fall to her and tell her my concerns. For several long minutes, I just answer questions, containing my impatience to be examined, and then, finally, the doctor puts gel on my belly and applies the scanner. The sound of a beating heart makes my own beat faster. The little being growing inside me is still there.

22
JEANNE

Each morning, Jeanne would take a little longer to leave her bed. The hours that followed, one after another until evening, seemed like so many insurmountable hurdles to her. Only her daily appointment with Pierre could revive her. For a few hours, her heart would function again. The rest of the time, she was an empty shell. The arrival of Iris and Théo hadn't helped matters. Their presence disturbed the absence that had taken over the apartment. She would wait until they had left for work to get up.

Emerging from her room this morning, Jeanne had the unpleasant surprise of finding Iris standing in the sitting room, cup in hand. The young woman didn't seem to hear her, so absorbed was she in studying a wedding photo of her and Pierre, displayed on the sideboard.

"You're not working?" Jeanne asked.

Iris jumped.

"The lady I look after in the morning is having tests done at the clinic. I start at one, at Monsieur Hamadi's. Would you like some tea?"

"No thanks."

"I'm so sorry, Jeanne. I didn't mean to be nosy. You're both so lovely in this picture."

Jeanne felt a lump in her throat. She knew every inch of that photo, just as she did of all those stuck in the albums piled up on her bedside table. She spent a considerable time trying to imprint her husband's smiling face on her memory. She did all she could to erase the image that had blotted out all the others: that final look in his eyes. It took up all the space, took over everything. This had become her greatest fear: that the happy memories would never resurface, and all that would remain was that day of June 15.

It was particularly lovely, that morning. Jeanne had opened the windows wide and planted her feet in the pool of light made by the sun on the parquet. From the turntable of the record player, which they couldn't bring themselves to replace with something more modern, Brel was singing "The Song of the Old Lovers," her favorite.

> *And every stick of furniture recalls*
> *In this room without a cradle*
> *The flashes of those old storms*
> *Nothing seemed the same anymore*

A suitcase lay open on the bed, still half-empty. In a few hours' time, she and Pierre would be setting off for Puglia, she mustn't dawdle. He'd gone out to get bread for the sandwiches. Reluctantly, she left the sunlight and went back to choosing the clothes she'd take with her. Since retiring, they traveled as much as they could. Never far, Pierre refused to fly—ostensibly out of concern for the planet, actually due to unbearable claustrophobia. They made do with vacations in France and the rest of Europe, and ended up seeing this limitation as fortunate, so enchanted were they by their various discoveries.

> *In the end, in the end*
> *It took quite some talent for us*
> *To be old without being grown up.*

This time, they were hiring a motorhome. They had already tried it out, in Scandinavia, with a group of other motorhomers, and it had turned out to be wonderful. The freedom this way of traveling gave them was exactly what they wanted. Jeanne was drawn from her thoughts by the sound of shouting. She went to the window to see where they were coming from and saw, some fifty meters away, a crowd on the pavement. Beyond the screen of onlookers, she could make out one man lying on the ground, and another performing cardiac massage on him. She understood before seeing, and ran straight for the door.

Oh, my love
My sweet, my tender, my marvelous love
From the clear dawn to the close of day
I still love you, you know

Pierre was unconscious when Jeanne got to him. She fell to her knees beside him, repeating his name like a prayer. A woman, phone in hand, told her she'd called for an ambulance, it was on its way. After what seemed like an eternity to her, Pierre opened his eyes. The young man stopped his massage and those watching applauded. Jeanne flooded her husband's face with kisses and tears.

"My love, I was so scared!"

"My head hurts," he whispered. "I'm scared of dying."

His eyes locked onto Jeanne's. That look she could no longer forget, full of terror and pain. His final look.

He breathed his last a few seconds later. What followed is still hazy in Jeanne's mind. The arrival of the ambulance, the attempts at resuscitation, the onlookers dispersing, the body being taken away, and her remaining alone there, on the pavement, frozen cold under the midday sun, a baguette lying at her feet.

I still love you, you know
I love you.

Suddenly, Jeanne moved in front of Iris and grabbed the framed photo from the sideboard, before returning to her room. The pool of sunlight flooded the parquet floor. Jeanne stood in it, pressing the photo to her heart, and wept until she could barely breathe.

23
THÉO

I've seen some right messes, but on this scale, never. Every time I open a drawer, it looks like burglars have rifled through it. You'd never think it, entering the apartment, it all looks spick and span. But don't open the cupboard, unless you want your brow busted by a Breton *bol*. I don't know how folk can live in chaos; personally, it sends me into a spin. This afternoon, Jeanne was out, as always, and Iris was in her room, so I decided to tidy up a bit. I took everything out, sorted it, classified it, cleaned it. I used to do the same at the kids' home when there was mess everywhere. At first, everyone took the piss out of me, but when fists started flying, they backed off. That's how it worked, I soon learned: you either let yourself be walked over, or do the walking over yourself. It's not the mess that really got to me, or the piss-taking, it's because it reminded me of my mother. At hers, it was a pigpen. I once heard that we all have a sun-resistance limit, and once reached, we must halt exposure to avoid health problems. At my mother's, I reached my mess-resistance limit. It was everywhere. She'd open a packet of cakes and chuck the wrapper onto the floor, she'd let the dirty dishes pile up, the floor was sticky, the bathroom gross. Occasionally, something would come over her, she'd have the music blaring, throw open all the windows and tidy everything up. She'd spend several days at it, filling up dozens of garbage bags, scrubbing the furniture, getting down on all fours to scrape away stubborn grime, washing heaps of dirty laundry, and I'd charge around with a feather duster, only too glad to be part of this big clean-up. Each time, I believed in it as if it were the first time. Each time, my illusions were shattered by real life.

"What are you doing?" Iris asks me, walking into the kitchen.

The crockery and the food are sorted into categories and I'm holding a sponge, but, apparently, she needs subtitles:

"I'm waxing my bikini line, isn't it obvious?"

She shrugs. I can't figure her out. She seems quite nice, for a woman who mistakes dachshunds for pit bulls and the stairs for a slide, but I can't forget that she tried to pull a fast one on me. I could have easily stayed on the street because of her. So, I can't help it, as soon as I see an opening, I have a dig at her.

She fills the kettle and comes up to me:

"Can I help you?"

"I'm nearly done."

"Want a tea?"

"Don't like it."

As she opens a box of tea, she lets out a chuckle:

"You need to ask your parents to go over basic politeness again."

I can feel my blood boiling in my veins, like whenever someone touches my sensitive spot. I stand up and look her straight in the eye:

"Do not speak of my parents."

Iris's reaction instantly defuses my anger. She steps back and puts her hands in front of her like a shield. Her lips are quivering. She mutters that it was a joke, that she didn't mean to upset me, and then goes off to her room, leaving the kettle whistling. I feel like an idiot. I didn't want to scare her, don't think I was aggressive, but that's how she took it. I must have spoken too loudly. I have a deep voice, so I've often been told. Maybe it alarmed her. I finish putting the plates away on the shelf and close the cupboard.

Iris opens her door as soon as I knock. Music escapes from her room, oldies' stuff no doubt, I don't recognize it. I hand her a steaming mug:

"I've made your tea for you. I'm sorry if I scared you."

"Thank you, that's nice. And I'm sorry for my rotten joke."

I don't know what to say next, so I ask the first question that comes to me:

"What are you doing?"

And back comes her inevitable reply:

"I'm shaving off my moustache, isn't it obvious?"

24
Iris

I close the door trying not to laugh. I didn't dare tell Théo, but his tea is undrinkable. He's thrown the loose leaves in the water instead of putting them in the tea ball. It's the first time in a month he's not unpleasant to me, I'd rather go without tea than break the spell.

My phone rings just as I'm about to go out. My mother, like every day since she discovered that I'd left. I don't answer. Her constant worrying really gets to me. That's why I didn't tell her: anxiety is my mother's lapdog, even more so since my father died. When it concerns me or my brother, it can easily veer into obsession. She'd calmed down once I was living with Jérémy. He was the reassuring, protective, and kind man she dreamed of for her only daughter. And contrary to my fears, she didn't even hold it against him that he'd taken me far away. I was in good hands, she could sleep easy.

During our last conversation, she told me he'd come to see her. It's not even him who told her I'd left, but his mother. "He's so considerate, he didn't want to cause me concern," she said. "I didn't recognize him, he's aged by ten years. You asked me not to give him your new number, I listened to you, but he's a pitiful sight, sweetie. You should at least get in touch with him, he's worried stiff."

I pictured Jérémy and my heart contracted. He's very thin-skinned, with a natural tendency to take everything personally. I thought back to when a rude remark from his boss had made him ill all weekend. To his constant need for reassurance. I felt bad for imposing this stifling uncertainty on him. But then I recalled one of the situations this emotional insecurity had led him into.

We'd just moved in together. After months of looking and several disappointments, I'd found a practice that needed a new physio to replace one who was retiring. The team, another physio and an osteopath—was exclusively female, a definite advantage in the eyes of Jérémy, who had worried when I was offered work at a practice run by a charming young man (who ended up withdrawing the offer at the last minute). I'd started my new job almost a week prior, and was finding my bearings with my patients and colleagues, both really nice. Jérémy was very attentive to my feelings and showered me with affection. He knew that leaving Bordeaux hadn't been easy, that I missed my family and friends. I'd suggested that he join me, but his position of property manager at a major bank wasn't the kind you give up lightly. From cycle rides in the old town to sunsets over the ocean, he'd managed to convince me that life in La Rochelle would be sweet. And it was, more than I'd imagined. My sky was an intense blue, without the slightest cloud on the horizon.

That morning, I didn't have to work. My first appointment was at two. But then Coralie, the other physio at the practice, had a problem and begged me to replace her for a few hours. Jérémy was working from home because his car was at the garage. I arrived slightly late, leapt out of the car and headed for the practice. A metallic sound stopped me in my tracks. I retraced my steps, convinced it came from my car. I walked right around it and was starting to think I was hearing things when I thought of opening the trunk. There was Jérémy, lying on his side, phone in hand. I remained rooted to the spot, as if in a state of shock, while he explained that he'd thought I was lying, that it wasn't his fault that I had a shifty look in my eye, that I had to be clearer with him, that he'd already been betrayed and didn't want it to happen again. I spent the day wondering what approach to take. That evening, he apologized and promised it would never happen again. He told me about his ex, who had cheated on him with his best friend, he cried. I felt truly sorry for him, and forgave him.

I delete the message from my mother without listening to it. I must protect myself, must protect *us*. Since yesterday, I can feel movements in my belly. Like little bubbles bursting. At first I thought it was Jeanne's stuffed cabbage, but I think it's the baby.

November

25
JEANNE

It was the first time Jeanne had seen so much activity at the cemetery. In front of the gate, a florist was selling pots of chrysanthemums. Jeanne shrugged. For her, every day was November 1.

"I'm so sorry I'm late, I went to visit my sister," she whispered to Pierre, stroking his photo on the marble.

"He doesn't seem to hold it against you," replied a female voice.

Jeanne looked around for the source and saw the woman from last time sitting on the bench. She pretended not to have heard this quip, which was tactless to say the least, and continued with her monologue:

"I hadn't visited Louise for a long time, today was the day. I promised her I'd be back soon. It's really near here, which is handy. Do you realize that Théo and Iris have been living at ours for exactly three weeks now? Well, believe it or not, I'm starting to get used to their presence. It doesn't feel as unbearable. Sure, I don't see much of them, they're often shut away in their rooms, but I sometimes find myself liking the company. Boudine does, too—terrorizing poor Iris is great fun."

The dog reacted to hearing its name by wagging its tail. Jeanne took a piece of paper out of her coat pocket and checked what was written on it before continuing:

"I turned the heating on. Last night, the temperature fell to eight degrees. Winter's going to be cold. The onions have put on several layers of skin, a sure sign. Talking of which, yesterday I made my first onion soup of the year. You so loved it . . . Iris enjoyed it, but the boy wouldn't touch it. I did offer to add some grated cheese, but he said he hated onions. For the past four or five days, we've all had supper together. To be more exact, we have supper side by side in front of the TV. It happened naturally, on the first evening, I'd simply forgotten that I wasn't cooking for us two anymore and had prepared a whole chicken, like we used to do it, with stock and roasted carrots. On the second evening, I hadn't forgotten that you weren't there anymore, but I still made a mushroom omelet that was far too much for me. Yesterday evening, Théo brought dessert, some chocolate eclairs he'd made. I told you he works at the bakery you got our bread from, didn't I? They couldn't put them on sale because the icing wasn't right, but that didn't stop us from gorging on them."

Jeanne went quiet for several seconds, then fished the paper out of her pocket again. For a while now, she'd been using the journey to jot down things she wanted to talk about with Pierre. They didn't come to her as spontaneously as at first, as if the spring were drying up. In fifty years of marriage, not once had she tired in the slightest of chatting with Pierre. When younger, the thought of sharing all of her life, and thus most of her conversations, with the same one person, had worried her. Weariness and repetition seemed unavoidable to her, so that she questioned whether she even wanted to get married. Meeting Pierre hadn't suddenly swept away her doubts, but, little by little, the desire to go through life with this man at her side had diminished them.

Jeanne was about to move on to the new lover of Monsieur Duval, on the second floor, when the woman on the bench butted in to her conversation once again.

"Has he been dead long?"

This time, Jeanne bothered to take a good look at the intruder. She was noticeably older than Jeanne, with short, blond hair under a black felt hat. She was openly smiling at her.

"Who are you?" asked Jeanne.

"Simone Mignot. My husband is tomb neighbor to yours.

I've come here every day for fifteen years, and am delighted to have alternative company to that of my dear husband, who, it must be said, isn't that chatty."

The exchange seemed so incongruous to Jeanne that she couldn't help but chuckle. She instantly regretted it, fearing she might have encouraged the woman. She didn't come there to have a natter, but to spend time with Pierre. This Simone seemed perfectly friendly, but she didn't need her prattling. To make her intentions quite clear, she blatantly turned her back on the woman and continued her hushed monologue. Nothing must mar her only moment of happiness each day.

26
THÉO

Philippe dives on me as soon as I walk through the door. In the time it takes to slip on my jacket, he's already spouted more words than in the whole time I've worked here. I struggle to follow, I'm still asleep. I concentrate to grasp what he's saying to me, and when I do, I regret having concentrated. Given the choice, I preferred it when my head was still up my ass.

"It's a new competition that rewards the best apprentice baker in Paris. I decided to enter you, the first heat is in two months, which allows time for practice. You'll only find out what's being tested at the last moment, but you can bet it'll be technique, so we're going to work on that between now and then. This morning we'll tackle St. Honoré cakes."

I wait until he's finished to tell him that he can count me out.

"I'm in my first year, I've not worked here even five months, I'll be slaughtered. It's out of the question."

Nathalie can't resist coming to give her opinion.

"If you're defeatist from the start, you'll definitely lose. Go on, it could be good publicity for us!"

"Have I really got the mug for a billboard?"

Leïla, standing just behind Nathalie, lets out a giggle. Nathalie blows a raspberry, just for a change. Never known anyone blow so many. She's like a butthole after a cassoulet. Philippe tries to convince me. He seems set on it, never seen him so fired up. They keep on at me, and it works, I end up agreeing to enter their competition. And everyone returns to what they were doing, as if they hadn't just made me shoulder a ton of stress.

I've already been in a competition. I was six years old. It had been three or four months since my mother had quit drinking, she'd found a job, never forgot to visit me, and the support workers were telling me I'd soon be able to live with her again. I was happy. There was this singing competition organized by the school, and being the one in my class who sang least out of tune, I was picked to represent it. The teachers and other pupils would vote, and the class of the person with the most votes would win. I was a bit nervous, especially since my mother had promised to be there. The support workers and kids from the home were in the audience. From the wings, I kept checking to see if she'd arrived in the hall, but no. I was disappointed, but didn't have much time to think about it. Corinne, my teacher, made me repeat the title of the song she'd chosen for me. It was "*Savoir aimer*" by Florent Pagny. I can still remember the words. It was my turn to sing, I walked onstage, scanned the audience and spotted her. She was sitting in the front row. I knew instantly that she'd been drinking. I could always tell from the first signs, I'd become a breathalyzer, and no need even to blow into it. I began to sing, she stood up, clapping and wolf-whistling. I tried not to look at her, but she staggered up to the stage and fell flat on her face trying to get up onto it. I started blubbing and ran off. As competition memories go, it's not the best.

I make choux buns and crème diplomate for a good hour, then go out to the little courtyard for a smoke. Something I rarely do, because they're not keen on us taking breaks as it is, but mainly because tobacco costs a bomb, so I've cut down. But right now, I need one.

"Can I cadge one off you?" Leïla asks, joining me.

It's the first time she's spoken to me. What with her working part-time and my days at the training center, I suppose we haven't had many opportunities.

I roll her a cigarette:

"Appreciate it, it's worth more than a diamond necklace."

What an idiot. She'll think I'm a skinflint.

She smiles:

"Maybe I'll wear it as a pendant then."

I watch her out of the corner of my eye as she lights it. I'd never noticed that brown spot on the white of her eye. She has long black eyelashes. Two teeth trying to jump over others. Bitten nails. Her hair's always tied back, for hygiene. I look away when she looks at me, but I do catch her blushing. I stay until the last drag, we don't exchange a word. Which is weird, because, for those few minutes, I feel like I've been close to her.

27
Iris

The day seemed never-ending to me. I hadn't counted the minutes like that since physics lessons in 10th grade.

My little occupant soaks up my energy and froths up my emotions. I have just one desire: to go home and take a shower, after a stop at Monoprix to buy some chestnut spread. I've been craving some for several days now.

I'm dithering between various options (with vanilla, with bits, in a pot or a tube) when I hear a familiar voice. My heart knows before I do, lurching in my chest. She's there, right beside me, I don't even need to look to know it's her. Mel. My oldest friend.

I was six when my parents moved to a small estate of five houses. Ours adjoined the garage. While they were lugging the furniture in, I went off to explore the garden. It seemed huge to me then. There wasn't yet any fencing, so I had the weird surprise of finding a little girl on our territory. I approached her, arms crossed and frowning, so she'd know who she was dealing with. She gave me a toothy, if gappy, smile and said her name was Mélanie. Our territories merged into one and I spent my childhood and adolescence between her home and mine, and later at Marie's and Gaëlle's, whose houses were added to the estate. I haven't seen Mel for over a year.

In the early days after I'd moved to La Rochelle, Mel, Marie, Gaëlle and I managed to keep in touch. We had a WhatsApp group in which we messaged every day. I returned rarely to Bordeaux, despite the promises I'd made on leaving, because Jérémy liked organizing romantic weekends. My friends understood. To begin with. The first snarky remark came after a canceled trip to Bordeaux. It was the second time it had happened, the first being due to Jérémy's back seizing up. For the second, he'd had to attend a last-minute work meeting. Marie implied that he was doing it on purpose. I thought she was joking, but she was serious, and the other two didn't contradict her. I took it badly, hurt that my friends could think badly of the guy I loved. And there was that time when it was them visiting me. They had rented a house two kilometers from our place, bringing husbands and kids along, too. Jérémy ate a dodgy oyster that first evening, and spent the weekend between his bed and the toilet.

"Would you like me to stay with you?" I asked him.

"I don't want to deprive you of your friends," he replied.

I was relieved. I missed the girls, and was happy to be able to spend time with them. I was away for two hours. On my return, he was in a right state. With the bowl—empty—sitting on his stomach, and his hair stuck to his forehead, he was groaning with every breath. I tried a joke, to lighten things up:

"Spread your legs, sir, I'm going to check how dilated you are."

He didn't laugh, but asked me to fetch some medication from the bathroom. He added that he'd wanted to go himself, but was in no condition to do so, and consequently had been in agony waiting for my return. I pulled out of the planned evening with my friends. When Marie suggested that they come over to ours, he said my friends were selfish and didn't deserve someone as generous as me.

A few days later, Gaëlle wrote a long message on WhatsApp. She was sharing her concerns with me about Jérémy's behavior, which she felt was domineering. The other two totally agreed with her. They all thought he was trying to distance me from my loved ones. Much as I tried to tell them about the Jérémy they didn't know—the considerate, sensitive and generous man I lived with—they wouldn't budge. "We love you, and know you're more fragile since the death of your father, he mustn't take advantage of that."

The WhatsApp messages became less frequent. I feared losing my friends. I organized a weekend at my mother's, Jérémy was all for it. I was keen for them to know this. Supper on the Saturday was at Mel's. She was in the middle of boxing everything up for her big move to Paris, where she'd found a job as a lawyer. She'd come across some old photos, which we all looked at and found hilarious. The memories kept coming: our gym classes, our goth get-ups at high school, the costume ball in 12th grade, celebrating my diploma, camping at Noirmoutier, going skiing, a pajama party at Marie's . . .

Jérémy was looking away. I tried to attract his attention, he didn't seem to hear me. Mel passed the album to him, he tossed it into the middle of the table. Everyone went quiet. I just looked at him, not understanding what might have annoyed him. I'd never seen him like that, his jaw tight and a furious look in his eye.

"They're just some old photos," Mel said. "There are no exes in them, if that's what you fear."

"Her previous life doesn't interest me," Jeremy retorted, coldly.

Marie grabbed my hand under the table and squeezed it.

"Why are you doing this?" I muttered. "We're having fun, there's no harm in it!"

He pushed back his chair and stood up abruptly:

"Right, come on, we're going."

Marie squeezed my hand tighter. Mel smiled at me:

"You can stay, Iris."

"We're here," Gaëlle added.

Jérémy made for the door:

"You do what you want, Iris. I'm going home. I won't tolerate a lack of respect."

I tried one last time to make him stay, but I already knew the outcome. So I muttered an apology to my friends, stood up and followed Jérémy.

For several weeks, I tried to explain Jérémy's reaction—and

my own. Marie replied briefly. Gaëlle sent an emoji. Mel remained silent.

I turn my head, Mel is there, a box of *biscottes* in her hand, her husband Loïc by her side. He spots me first. I freeze, but he seems pleased. He smiles at me and nudges Mel, whose eyes follow his and land on me. In them I can see that she's surprised, quite pleased, very embarrassed. Reassured, I move towards her with arms out to hug her, as we always used to. But those days are over. Before I can reach her, Mel grabs a jar of jam, turns on her heel and walks off without a word.

28
JEANNE

Jeanne received another letter. The envelope felt thicker than usual. Upon opening it, she understood why: a photograph cut out from a newspaper accompanied the missive. As she recognized it, her hands started to shake.

Winter 1997

It's snowing in Paris. This is rare, and it splits the city into two clans: those who are delighted and those who moan. Jeanne and Pierre are among the former. The pristine scene makes them feel as if they're on vacation at home. Wearing boots bought for the occasion, they head to Montmartre, which seems to have been turned into an impromptu winter-sports resort. It's a wonderful sight: children sliding down on garbage bags, and the bravest having brought along their skis. Pierre suggests they try sledding down, Jeanne is totally against the idea. "No way. We're fifty years old, not twenty, I'd remind you!" A few minutes later, that same Jeanne, sitting between her husband's legs on a garbage bag that's hurtling down the slope, shrieks with joy.

When Iris got home, she found Jeanne asleep on the sofa. She was gently snoring, with Boudine lying beside her. The dog leapt up to welcome Iris, waking its mistress. Jeanne folded the letter that was still in her hand and slipped it under the belt of her dress.

"Are you alright?" asked Iris, concerned.

"I just felt a little tired, I feel better now," Jeanne assured her, standing up. "Would you like an aperitif? I must still have some Suze, some Martini, or some port. We liked the occasional tipple, Pierre and I."

"I'll have an orange juice, thanks."

Iris went to hang up her coat in the hall, then added, gently:

"I don't want to seem nosy, but neither do I want you to think I'm not interested in you. Pierre was your husband?"

"Yes," whispered Jeanne.

"Has he been gone a while?"

"Four months."

"Oh! It's recent . . . I'm so sorry."

"It's an eternity."

Jeanne placed two glasses on the table.

"I can't seem to accept that he's no longer of this world. That expression takes on its full meaning when you're faced with it. 'No longer of this world.' I could look for him everywhere, move heaven and earth, travel the planet, but I wouldn't find him. He's no longer part of my existence."

Her voice faltered. She sat down beside Iris and drank a gulp of Suze.

"And you, have you ever encountered love?" she asked Iris.

The young woman looked down.

"I don't know. I thought I had, but I'm no longer sure."

A jangling of keys interrupted the conversation. The door opened and Théo walked into the apartment. He looked surprised to discover his two roommates sitting at the table with a drink, and greeted them from a distance.

"Would you like something to drink?" Jeanne asked him. "An orange juice, grenadine syrup? I might have some mint syrup, too . . . "

"I am eighteen, you know!" the young man said, amused. "I can show you my identity card."

Jeanne smiled:

"You're a baby, but since you insist, I have some port, some Suze and some Martini."

"O.K. . . . so I've landed in the last century . . . there's no beer?"

Since the drinks offered didn't appeal to him, Jeanne gave him a glass of pear brandy and put a few savory snacks on a plate and some olives in a ramekin. Théo grimaced as he drank his aperitif. Iris cooked a squash gratin, which they all enjoyed together. The young man spoke of his passion for patisserie, the young woman told anecdotes about the people she looked after. The TV remained switched off. Jeanne took Boudine outside a bit later than usual, feeling slightly tipsy after the two glasses of Suze, and all that new life around her table. Before closing the door behind her, she turned to Iris and Théo, who were busy clearing the table:

"How about we all go from '*vous*' to '*tu*?'"

29
THÉO

Once a month, I walk through the big gate. I don't like that gate, in either direction. I don't like coming, and I like leaving even less.

I had to take the train—it was easier when I lived nearby. I dozed off, almost missed my stop. I'm pooped, I've been hitting the sack really late because of the competition. I practice every evening at the apartment. Two people aren't complaining, Iris even had seconds and thirds of my opera cake.

The woman in reception doesn't even check me out, anyone can walk in here. But then, who would come here without having to?

I take a deep breath before opening the door. I always do, as if it changed anything. It gains me a few seconds, which I suppose is something.

My mother is in her room. They've put her in the armchair. I straighten her head, as it's lolling to one side. It's dumb, but every time I open that damn door, I hope she's going to smile at me. And yet the doctors were clear: no chance she'll get better. It's my mother's body, but she's no longer really inside it. I'm not even sure she's aware of my presence.

They say she was lucky, that she could have died on the spot. Becoming a vegetable at forty-three, I don't call that lucky. All that's lucky is that she didn't kill anyone in the car opposite. It was five years ago, and I can't get over it.

I sit on her bed and take out my phone, but it's my thoughts I'm scrolling through. I can't help imagining how our lives would have been if my mother hadn't been an alcoholic. I got a few glimpses, on the occasions when she quit drinking. I even went back to live with her twice, she was sure of herself, the messing around was over. I truly believed it. She was a different person. We had good fun, she was forever singing and dancing, she loved to cook, especially baking cakes, she'd take me to build dens in the forest or at the beach, even though it was a three-hour drive away. She couldn't care less if I missed school, she'd say that you don't learn about life sitting down. She often slept in my bed, sometimes because I asked her to, sometimes because she felt like it. She'd write me little notes that she stuck around the apartment, to tell me that she loved me, that I was the greatest little boy, that I was her sunshine. I kept them, they're in the car at the pound. And then, suddenly, just like that, for no apparent reason, she went back to drinking. And not just a little. She drank from waking up until she couldn't walk straight anymore, couldn't speak clearly anymore. She drank straight from the bottle. She drank secretly, at first, then in the sitting room, in my bedroom, in the street. She'd lose her job. She wouldn't cook anymore, sing anymore, dance anymore. She'd go to the gas station in the middle of the night to buy booze. She'd want to leave me at home, but I'd beg her to take me with her. I was too scared she'd kill herself on the road. I'd straighten the steering wheel when we were veering off it. She'd forget to take me to school. She'd forget to take me when she set off with friends for the weekend. Even if we moved, there were always neighbors who'd end up reporting her. When social services turned up, I'd deny everything.

If I'd been there, I'd have straightened that steering wheel. What gets me most is that there won't be another last chance.

I stay all afternoon, trying to solve our world's problems in my head. Each time I leave, it's the same ritual. I kiss her on the cheek, tell her that I've never held it against her, that it wasn't her fault, that fucking illness, I read the text pinned to the wall, which they found in her wallet after the accident, and promise her I'll be back soon.

I walk through the big gate. I don't like it, in either direction. I don't like coming, and I like leaving even less.

30
IRIS

When I enter Madame Beaulieu's, I'm surprised not to be greeted by my charming nickname. The sitting room is empty, her daughter's voice asks me to join her in the bedroom. I find her in the middle of filling a bag with items of clothing and toiletries.

"My mother has just left in an ambulance. I'm so sorry, Iris, in all the confusion I didn't think to call the agency to warn you. You've come for nothing. I'm just off to join her."

"What happened?"

She's in a state, her hands are shaking, and her cheeks are still tear-stained.

"We were having breakfast, I saw her mouth twist and what she was saying made no sense, the words were coming out jumbled. I called for an ambulance, it arrived promptly. They think it's a stroke, they're going to do all the tests on her."

Words seem vain in such circumstances, but I know, from having felt it, that each one is a little salve on the wound. I received numerous messages of support after my father died. A few lines, sometimes a few pages, an email, text messages, from those close to me and less close. I read them, and reread them, again and again, drinking in the love they conveyed. Ever since, I'm totally convinced that, when the heart is an open wound, it receives love in an animal-like, almost savage way. It attracts it, seizes it and feeds on it. It transcends it. All the rest becomes trivial. It's all that counts. Words, smiles, caresses, others.

So I tell her that my thoughts are with her, and I hope things will be alright. That her mother is a remarkable woman, who has often made me laugh, and sometimes moved me. That I'm really pleased to know her. That I hope to see her again soon, and hear her calling me "little tart." The daughter laughs and cries at the same time.

I stay on after she's gone to tidy up and clear the table of the interrupted breakfast. The words of the trainer, at the agency, about being a care worker come back to me. We're admitted into people's private life, we sometimes become their sole human interaction, and affection is sometimes inevitable.

I leave a note on the table to wish a happy return to Madame Beaulieu, and leave the apartment thinking of all the patients I left behind in La Rochelle.

I didn't choose the job of physiotherapist randomly. I wanted to repair humans. This vocation may have begun at the age when I'd dislocate the arms of my Barbies, or when my grandmother would ask me to massage her back, but the fact remains that I don't recall ever wanting to do anything else. I was lucky to find work as soon as I'd finished my studies. Realizing a dream inevitably runs the risk of disappointment. And yet, from the first minute of my first day, I knew I was doing exactly what I was meant to do. I rapidly specialized in childhood motor issues. It was when giving muscular, neurological or respiratory therapy that I felt truly grateful. I haven't practiced for nearly five months. I feel, by visiting Madame Beaulieu, Monsieur Hamadi, Nadia and the others, that I'm continuing to repair humans, and yet I miss my real profession. I miss my patients. For a few days now, I've been looking at job ads, some could be right for me, but I refrain from applying. In a little over two months, I'll be on maternity leave, but maybe I'll take the plunge afterwards. Maybe afterwards, I'll no longer fear him phoning every physio practice to find me.

31
JEANNE

Jeanne was annoyed: Simone Mignot was already on the bench. She greeted her half-heartedly, not even deigning to look at her. A bus breaking down had made her late, she didn't intend to lose a second more of her time with Pierre. Unfortunately, his tomb-neighbor's wife wasn't having it.

"Isn't the weather simply glorious?"

Jeanne, not wanting to forget her manners, managed an entirely neutral response, praying that that would satisfy her assailant's hunger for chit-chat.

"Hello, my love," she whispered, so as not to be heard. "So sorry I'm late, I thought I'd never get here. I almost continued on foot, but I wore my little heels today, and you know I can't walk for long in them."

"That's why I only wear flats," Simone commented. "But apparently they're not great for the back, so who knows what's best."

Jeanne pretended not to hear, took her list of conversation topics out of her pocket, glanced at it, and continued:

"I had coffee with Victor this morning. Hadn't done so for some time. He's done up the caretaker flat nicely, I'm sure his mother would have liked it. Although, thinking about it, it might be too sober for her. She liked colors and frills."

"Personally, I favor white. I find there's nothing more elegant than white walls, with a few framed pictures hung on them. Ideally, black and white. My daughter-in-law loves everything shiny, I'm almost blinded every time I visit. I go there for my grandchildren—if I had to wait for them to visit me, I'd be mummified. Do you have grandchildren?"

Annoyance trumped politeness. Jeanne turned to Simone:

"Madame, can you not see that I'm talking to my husband? Would you kindly keep out of our conversation?"

"Oh, I'm so sorry!" spluttered the woman in the hat. "I don't often get the chance to talk, so when an occasion presents itself, I forget my manners."

Jeanne returned to her moment with her husband, but a cloud hung over it now. Her parents had brought her up to respect others, even to the detriment of respecting oneself. And that was without her excessive empathy, which sometimes made her disregard her own feelings. She had rarely put her desires to the fore, and whenever she had, an intense feeling of guilt had followed. She felt bad for Simone, alone on her bench, rebuffed by a stranger. So she explained the situation to Pierre in her quietest voice, and went to sit beside Simone, followed by Boudine.

Simone didn't bother to play it cool, happy to have a willing listener.

Her husband, Roland, had been dead for fifteen years. She missed him as much now as ever, like a lost limb. She lived with the constant feeling of having lost something, and came to the cemetery to look for it.

"Every day for fifteen years, I've not skipped a single visit!" she insisted. "Even when I had my endoscopy, they wanted to keep me there all day, I signed the discharge form to get out. I don't regret any of it, I'm happy this way. He's still with me a little, know what I mean?"

Jeanne knew only too well. Visiting Pierre was her only reason for continuing to live.

Simone was nicer than first impressions had suggested. Jeanne enjoyed their chat, but still didn't delay returning to her husband.

Simone had gone when Jeanne left the cemetery. She reached the bus stop just as the doors were closing. The driver spotted her at the last moment and let her get on. With Boudine lying at her feet, she gazed at the buildings, the pedestrians, the cars, the store windows. Some had already put up Christmas decorations. Everything went so fast.

When Jeanne got in, she found Théo and Iris in the kitchen. The young man had brought home some equipment to practice.

"I'm going to make you a St. Honoré cake!" he announced, proudly.

Jeanne smiled, said she urgently needed the bathroom, and went and locked herself in. There, she stood in front of the mirror and studied herself for a long time. Nothing showed, nothing was visible. And yet Simone had put into words what Jeanne felt. For four months, she'd been missing a limb.

32
THÉO

I'm not sure I'm cut out for karate, and even less sure karate's cut out for me. Whenever we move into combat mode, I make sure I end up with Sam, the ten-year-old. But the instructor must have smelt a rat, so he put me opposite Laurent, a guy who's two heads taller than me and has shoulders I could do the splits on. Only the fenders are missing to mistake him for a 4x4. He's not a man, he's scaffolding. A wardrobe with feet and arms. But a large wardrobe, right, the sort Beyoncé would have. When he positions himself in front of me, I hesitate to ask him if I should shake his hand or pull the door handle, but I soon get that he's not there to mess around.

At the end of the lesson, I understand why they make us wear some protection. If I hadn't worn the box, I'd have scrambled eggs in my shorts. As I pull on my sneakers, trying not to groan, I spot Sam smiling.

"You wouldn't be laughing at me, would you?"

He laughs:

"Just a bit, I admit."

It's dark and cold when we all file out. Everyone scatters, doors slam and engines start up. Sam says goodbye and goes to get his bike, chained at the side of the hall. I was about to set off for the metro home, but I see him struggling.

"Fuck, bunch of bastards, they've let down my tires!"

I refrain from mentioning his bad language—at his age I was no model of politeness. At the kids' home, you have to show you're big and tough, especially when you're small and weak. Have to make a noise and take up space. Mustn't reveal a flaw, or there'll be those who'll pounce on it. Swearing and hitting, they're like epaulettes. They give you the stature you lack. At ten, I dealt out the insults and the blows while waiting to be big enough not to need them.

"Can your parents come and pick you up?"

"No, but I don't live far, I'll push the bike to mine, it's no big deal."

"I'll come with you."

"There's no need."

"You're a kid, it's dark, I'm not letting you walk home alone."

He talks the whole way. About his little sister who's three, and funny except when she pinches his toys. About Minecraft, his favorite game, but his father won't let him play during the week. About his cat Charlot, who's slept in his bed since he was little. About his friend Marius, who brought cigarettes to school. About his impatience to start 6th grade. Of karate, which he loves, even if he likes hip-hop dancing, too. About his bike, that's already been stolen twice. He barely catches his breath, he talks, and talks, and talks, in a voice that hovers between shrill and hoarse, wavers between childhood and adolescence. He makes me laugh, with his very own way of speaking. He slips lots of old-folk expressions into his childish sentences, among the swearwords.

"Marius I've known since nursery school, he's my best friend. Sometimes he's a pain in the butt, but I always forgive him, I can take the rough with the smooth."

Or:

"Honestly, I'm fucking sick of people messing with my bike, it just beggars belief."

I don't refrain from laughing, which only encourages him.

It takes us more than ten minutes to get there, the kid must have meant the time it took *on* his bike. He pulls a bunch of keys out of his bag and thanks me for accompanying him. I wait until he's closed the door behind him before walking back to get my metro. From my phone, I send a text message to Jeanne and Iris: "I'll be a bit late, don't worry."

33
Iris

Madame Beaulieu is dead. They managed to stabilize her after the first stroke, but three days later, a second one got her. The agency manager let me know, and reassured me: she would send me to someone else to replace her, an elderly lady with Parkinson's. Feeling awkward, I evaded the subject. Of course, Madame Beaulieu did represent a significant part of my income, but, when she'd just passed away, it wasn't my immediate concern. A little later, her daughter sent me a message thanking me for my support of her mother. I replied with a few pathetically trite lines, not daring to tell her how sad I really was, how I really did know what she was suffering.

Nadia is in bed when I enter her apartment. Her son is sitting beside her, engrossed in *In Search of Lost Time*.

"He didn't go to school," she explains. "He saw that I was weak and didn't want to leave me on my own."

"He's reading Proust at ten years old, I think he can miss one or two days of school. Have you seen the doctor?"

"Yes, this morning. It's my MS again. My legs won't carry me anymore, I have to use the wheelchair. I'm sick and tired of it, I've just bought myself a little dress and I'll never manage to put it on!"

"I can help you!"

She laughs:

"It's too short, when sitting down, the view of my privates will be unrestricted. And I won't be able to take it off on my own. I'm doomed to wear tunics that are comfortable and easy to put on, but make me look like an old lady."

"Sorry, Mom, but you're no spring chicken anymore," Léo chimes in.

"Thanks, darling! I'm only thirty-six, you know."

"Just as I said," the boy deadpans, trying not to smile.

Nadia impresses me with her acceptance of the illness, and her resilience. She doesn't jump over obstacles, she sweeps them away. She reminds me of the children I treated at the practice in La Rochelle, their joie de vivre whatever the ordeal, even that of illness. It wasn't unusual for me to get home in the evening emotionally drained by the unfairness of Mother Nature. Jérémy would listen to me, comfort me, and repeat to me how admirable my work was. He worried, even, wondering if I was tough enough, thought I risked harming myself. I remember one evening in particular, when I'd told him of my sadness at the dismal prognosis for little Lucas, just six years old. Jérémy had hugged me tight and stroked my head:

"My darling, you have many qualities, but you're far too sensitive for that job. You don't think little Lucas would have sensed your distress? You think you're helping him? I'm sorry if I'm being a bit blunt, but someone has to tell you. You're not cut out for it, and you're doing more harm than good."

He had undermined a part of me that I thought was unshakeable. Never had I questioned my vocation, my professionalism, and my usefulness. I was plagued with doubt in many areas, but never remotely in that one. And yet Jérémy's words had eroded my certainty. Worst of all, I preferred to believe that he was right rather than think he might want to do me down.

"The doctor thinks that this time I won't recover," Nadia says, while I help her out of bed. "I'm only fit for a life on four wheels now!"

"The dream!" her son exclaims. "I hate walking, you're *so* lucky!"

Nadia bursts into laughter, and Léo comes to snuggle up to her. Like her, he wields derision like a sharp weapon. I observe the two of them, doubtless as distressed as each other by this latest attack of the illness, I see them making immense efforts not to let resignation win, overcoming the challenges hand in hand, while taking care not to drag each other down into their own anguish. I admire this scene of a mother and her child, and tell myself that everything is possible. Nadia once told me that Léo's father had just vanished while she was pregnant. She had tracked him down and insisted that he recognize his son, convinced that fear was going to deprive Léo's father of great happiness. He let himself be persuaded, but disappeared again when the baby was three months old, never to give another sign of life.

I'm going to have a child on my own. Like many women before me. We will be happy. I promise us.

DECEMBER

34
Jeanne

Jeanne had always been scared of spiders, especially when they could almost be mistaken for crabs. So, when she spotted the creature on the sitting-room wall, she froze and let out a cry worthy of a goat.

Iris ran into the room, almost tripping over Boudine. She stopped dead in front of the monster.

"What the hell is that thing?"

"I'm inclined to think it's a spider," Jeanne replied.

"But it's massive!"

"You said it. I don't know how we're going to get out of this fix. Can you grab the broom?"

"I can grab it, but no way am I taking it near that thing. Don't you think it looks shifty? It'll jump on me. I'm not going there."

Then Théo turned up. He let out an admiring whistle at the sight of the spider. Relieved, Jeanne saw him as her savior.

"Ah, Théo! Can you get rid of this thing for us?"

"Of course," said the young man. "Got a flame-thrower?"

"Of course not."

"Then I can't do a thing."

Iris gave Théo a suspicious look:

"You're scared of spiders?"

"I'm not scared, bullshit. I'm just wary of anything that has more legs than me."

"Théo, can you go get the vacuum cleaner?" Jeanne pleaded.

"It's in the kitchen, isn't it?"

"Yes, beside the fridge."

"To get there, I'll have to go through that door. In case you haven't noticed, the tarantula is just above it."

Iris let out a nervous laugh, which turned into a groan when the spider edged towards the corner of the wall.

"Oh my god!" Jeanne screamed, while Théo bravely took three steps backwards.

It was Iris who decided to go fetch the caretaker. By the time he arrived, the creepy-crawly had managed to cross the sitting room. Victor found Jeanne and Théo transfixed at the opposite end of the room, their eyes riveted on the dark form.

"If I just take my eyes off it," Jeanne wailed, "it's going to escape and we'll have to live knowing that a monster might be sharing our bed."

The man captured the spider inside a clear plastic box, to the screams of those watching. Then said he'd release it outdoors, rather than kill it.

"Not less than three hundred kilometers from here, Victor!" Jeanne ordered.

"Of course," he replied. "Maybe I should get it a train ticket."

He returned ten minutes later to reap the effusive thanks of the three roommates—and drink to the disappearance of the intruder.

"It seems to be going well," he said, finishing his drink. "I mean, the three of you living together, it seems to be going well?"

Iris agreed:

"We get on nicely, and we respect each other. It's tricky, getting one's bearings in a new place, but I'm really starting to feel at home."

"You lived in Paris before?" he asked.

"No, in the provinces."

Jeanne noticed Iris stiffening and came to her aid:

"It's going better than I could have hoped. I only regret that Théo isn't tidier. But the young are like that . . . "

Théo almost choked, before realizing that the old lady was teasing him. He wasn't used to her doing that. Lately, Jeanne's sense of humor had been resurfacing.

"I'm sorry if I was a bit blunt with you on the first day," Victor said to Théo. "Jeanne means a lot to me, and I was worried about her being at the mercy of strangers."

"No worries, bro."

Victor stayed for supper. Jeanne hastily made some mashed parsnips and cod fillets, and Théo baked an apple crumble. Once Victor had left and Iris gone to bed, Théo offered Jeanne to take Boudine out.

"I fancy a smoke, I might as well walk her."

Jeanne said it was fine, she needed to stretch her legs. They went down together, into the silence of the night.

The cold formed clouds of vapor in front of their mouths. They walked slowly towards the park at the end of the street. When Théo lit a cigarette, Jeanne seized it and put it to her lips.

"You smoke?" Théo asked, astonished.

"No," Jeanne replied, coughing, before taking another drag. "I always refrained, having seen the ravages of smoking on my poor grandfather. But it always appealed to me. At my age, I'm not risking a thing anymore by starting, am I?"

She held the white stick away from her mouth to contemplate it, took another drag, and returned it to Théo:

"Shame it's so disgusting."

35
THÉO

Everyone's more motivated than me at the bakery. Philippe makes me work morning to night, and, most notably, Nathalie speaks nicely to me. It doesn't seem natural, it's like she's moving her lips and someone's dubbing her. What I like most is when Leïla encourages me. Whenever I've finished a new cake, she tells me it's great, and that makes me want to bake plenty more great cakes.

I like the days when she's there. They're like the other days, but sometimes she smiles at me, and I feel my cheeks burn. I mustn't kid myself, there's no way she'd be interested in me. It would be great if, one day, I stopped getting attached at the slightest sign of interest. And yet I know that it's not worth the effort. Every time I've given a piece of my heart, I've got it back in an awful state. Better to have no one, at least there's no risk of losing my heart then.

Manon used to tell me that she'd love me forever, and I believed her. I should have known, seeing as my mother played the same trick on me. Manon and I had loads of plans for when we'd be free, once we were both eighteen. We'd even chosen a name for our cat. We'd been together for nearly two years, in fact, at the kids' home, everyone spoke of us as if we were a single person. "Manon'n'Théo." When I caught her snogging Dylan, I thought I was going to die. It had the same effect on me as when I'd catch my mother drinking when she'd quit. Manon didn't even attempt to apologize—I was too nice, and she'd fallen in love, she couldn't help it, over, end of story. And with Dylan, of all people. I thought I was seeing things. I'm not the sort to criticize looks, but there's a limit. That guy, it's not teeth he's got, it's a grand piano. It didn't last, and even if I'd never admit it, I think I could have gone back with her if she'd wanted it. She didn't want it. I was eighteen two months later, so I left. That's the rule: at eighteen, you clear off, but even without that, I wouldn't have stayed a second more. Honestly, I have some good memories, we had fun times, and I made some real friends, especially Ahmed and Gérard. But make no mistake, you're not there for the pleasure of it. Generally, you're pretty damaged when you arrive, so there's quite a bit of violence, and when you're damaged, you need everything but violence. Ahmed and Gérard have phoned me several times, I've never replied. When I arrived in Paris, I wanted to begin a new life and hear nothing of the old one anymore. But it's no good, part of me still lingers back there.

"What are you doing?" Leïla asks me, coming up to my worktop.

"I'm stuffing some *religieuses*," I reply, seizing a choux bun to pipe in some crème pâtissière.

She bursts out laughing:

"A weird thing to say!"

It takes me a few seconds to understand, and then I laugh with her. Nathalie arrives like a charging rhinoceros:

"Leïla, what are you doing?"

"I was going to take the *pains au chocolat* out of the oven."

"You're wasting lots of time, you need to get going! The window's not going to dress itself."

Leïla rolls her eyes discreetly and heads for the oven. I return to my *religieuses*. Nathalie can't resist a parting shot:

"I don't know what's going on between you two, but we're in a bakery here, not on a dating site."

36
Iris

The ultrasound department is on the ground floor of the hospital. I register at reception and take a seat in the waiting room. I might have heard its heartbeat recently, but I'm still anxious. It's not just a child growing inside me, it's a promise. I might tell myself not to get attached to it before its born, but the fact is, I already love it to distraction.

I grew up with someone missing. I was five when my brother Clément was born, eight when my mother's stomach swelled again. It was a girl, she was named Anaïs, and I hated seeing her move beneath the taut skin of my mother's belly, it disgusted me. When my mother went off to the hospital, I prepared a box containing gifts for my little sister: a security blanket I had no use for, a doll I had no use for, barrettes I had no use for. I was generous with the stuff I had no use for. My father got home first, he told us the news. I remember the long hug he gave us, my brother and me, and the sobs that shook him. I cried just once, when my mother got home. I wouldn't have that little sister I'd imagined playing at Barbie or Four in a Row with the minute she arrived. We've never forgotten her, she's part of every birthday celebration, every Christmas, we often speak of her, and every April 24, my mother spends all day crying over her. And yet I've never fully appreciated the tragedy that rocked my parents' lives. Never, until today. I now know how much you can love someone you don't yet know. I know what you're capable of doing to protect a little being who depends on you. I know that if I lost it, I'd never get over it.

A nurse takes me to the examination room and tells me the

radiologist won't be long. I try to relax while waiting. There are fifty-six tiles on the ceiling, two of which are stained.

A young man greets me as he enters the room. If he weren't in a white coat, I'd ask him if he'd lost his parents. He looks about twelve. I hesitate to ask him for ID as he pours the gel onto my stomach.

"It's the morphology?"

"Sorry?"

"It's the scan at twenty-two weeks? The morphology scan?"

"Yes, yes, that's right."

"So, we're going to look at all the organs and see if the baby's developing well. Here we go."

The doctor explores every centimeter of my stomach with the scanner. His eyes don't leave the screen, and my eyes don't leave his face. I try to interpret the slightest frown, the merest pout. He says nothing, and I don't dare ask a single question, for fear of seeming like the anxious mother that I'm obviously not.

"Ah," he suddenly says.

"What?"

"That's not right."

My blood freezes. I stop breathing, maybe if I pretend to be dead, fate will forget me?

"The software's malfunctioning," he finally says. "We've just got the machine back, they're supposed to have repaired it, but nothing's changed. I won't be able to do any 3D images, I'm afraid."

If he knew how little I care, at this moment in time, about 3D images. My blood flows in my veins once more and, as if to reassure me, the baby does a somersault.

"Ah, perfect!" the radiologist exclaims. "I was waiting for it to turn. Would you like to know its sex?"

I don't hesitate for a second.

Half an hour later, I leave the hospital hugging a file to my chest that contains not a 3D image, but one of a tiny willy I want to show to the whole world.

37
JEANNE

When she walked through the medium's door for the second time, Jeanne had set aside any doubts. After brief reflection, she had concluded that she had two options: either she believed in an afterlife with Pierre, or she believed in an eternity without Pierre. As she settled onto Bruno Kafka's divan, she congratulated herself for having chosen the first option. Life was more bearable if it wasn't mortal.

"I'm pleased to see you again," the medium said, in welcome.

"Thanks for letting me know that Pierre wanted to talk to me again. Is he here?"

The man closed his eyes and seemed to concentrate, before smiling:

"Pierre is among us. He finds you very beautiful."

Jeanne blushed. She had enjoyed getting herself ready, like for their first dates. Accompanied by Jacques Brel's voice, she had wound a ribbon around her chignon, enhanced her cheeks and lips with a pink tint, and touched up her lashes. She was wearing a midnight-blue dress that Pierre had bought for her in a little boutique in Rome, and the black-silk lingerie that made him go wild, hoping that death had given him the power to see through clothes. She had hesitated over this, fearing she was being tacky, but their bodies had loved as much as their souls, and she thought he'd appreciate the gesture.

"He's proud of you," the man continued. "He thinks you're very strong."

Jeanne thought that if strength consisted of crying ten liters of tears every night and holding back ten liters of tears every day, then sure, she was strong.

"Pierre wants you to know that he's by your side. He sees you."

A shiver ran through Jeanne. Sometimes—often—she found herself imagining her husband by her side. If she really concentrated, she could feel his breath on her skin. The man was confirming that she wasn't crazy. She had had qualms about returning, due to the cost of the consultation, but entertaining the hope that Pierre was still there, somewhere, waiting for her, was certainly worth two hundred euros.

"Has he met up with his brother?" asked Jeanne. "And his dear parents?"

The medium rolled his eyes and let out a grunt. Jeanne hoped he wasn't having a heart attack, or that at least he'd manage to answer her first.

"He has met up with all your departed loved ones. I see him surrounded by elderly people and younger people. His parents seem to be alongside him, is that right?"

Jeanne struggled to swallow. She silently nodded, perturbed by the image that had come to her. On the sideboard in the hall, in pride of place since forever, there had been a photo of Pierre as a child flanked by his parents. Imagining them reunited once more really moved her.

The medium returned to earth:

"We're done. It was very intense. I think we'll need to see each other again, do you agree?"

Despite the brevity of each séance, Jeanne agreed without a moment's hesitation. She could surely scrape together enough money from the few bits of jewelry she owned. She noted down the appointment in her diary, put on her coat, and thanked the man warmly.

"Pierre sends you all his love," he assured her, holding open the door. "You and your children."

38
Théo

When I got back from work, earlier, the two old girls were waiting for me. At first I was pleased, I'm not used to anyone waiting for me, it made me feel like I had a family. But my pleasure went the same direction as Iris on the stairs when I realized they were just waiting for me to do them a favor. If I've got it right, Iris told Jeanne about a woman who didn't have any suitable clothes to wear in her wheelchair, and, snap, Jeanne lit up like a Christmas tree and asked if we could go down to the cellar and bring up a few things.

Iris grips the handrail as if trying to get milk out of it. She seemingly doesn't fancy starring in a remake of *Cool Runnings*.

I didn't even know there was a cellar. The moment we open the door leading down to it, the caretaker pops out of his flat. He does that whenever anyone goes by, he's not a man, he's a champagne cork.

"Everything okay?"

"Kinda," I reply. "We need a little help, are you free?"

"Of course, to do what?"

"We're going to hide Jeanne's limbs in the cellar, could you take care of the legs?"

It works like a dream. He turns as white as his teeth, and I nearly lost a retina the first time he flashed them. Iris explains to him that it's a joke, he guffaws, saying he obviously knew that.

I go down first, not out of chivalry, just so there's no hanging about. I hate basements, they make me feel like I'll get trapped and suffocate to death. It's one of my worst nightmares, I've had it since I was small. There's also the one where I'm being chased, but I run on the spot and not a sound comes from my mouth when I cry out. At the home, I'd hung a dream-catcher, which Manon made for me, above my bed. For a few weeks, I didn't dream. I don't know what was working: the dream-catcher, or the fact that someone loved me enough to make me one. I left it back there, thinking there was no reason my nightmares would follow me into my new life. But it sure looks like they've tracked me down.

I have the key ready. We reach the door, I quickly open it. The cellar is small. Sheets cover what Jeanne has stored there. Iris moves in front of me and lifts the fabric:

"Jeanne said it was against the right-hand wall."

We find some wooden shelves.

"The sewing machine's right there," says Iris. "The cardboard boxes, too. She also mentioned a worktable, can you see it?"

Not being sure what that is, I say no and pretend to look for one. I reach out to check under another sheet, against the wall opposite.

"Théo! Jeanne didn't seem to want us poking around anywhere else. She repeated several times that we must look on the right."

I try to put the sheet back in place, but, too late, it's come loose and slips to the floor. Iris quickly picks it up and we put it back as best we can, but we both had time to see the cradle, with a big, fawn teddy bear lying inside it.

39
Iris

It's the first time I'm walking in Paris for a reason other than getting to work or doing shopping. I'm strolling, aimlessly, simply for the pleasure. I'm moving away from my refuge, leaving my comfort zone, and it makes me feel giddy. All these people, all these faces, all these bodies rushing around. I so loved crowds before. I liked things to be busy, move forward, be vibrant. My parents lived in the distant suburbs of Bordeaux, a house on an estate surrounded by vineyards. My mother often went into town for work, and I'd beg her to take me with her, and feel like I was discovering the world. As a teenager, I'd take the bus with Mel, Marie and Gaëlle to go and listen to CDs at the Virgin Megastore on Place Gambetta, before heading for Place de la Victoire along Rue Sainte-Catherine. We'd have a coffee at Auguste's, then return to what we called our back-of-beyond. During my studies, I lived with Mel in an apartment behind the Cours d'Alsace-et-Lorraine. Thanks to my room's single glazing, I'd hear the cars and voices as if my bed were on the pavement. After a few nights, I could drop the earplugs I'd been using for years. The silence deafened me more than the noise.

Jérémy didn't grow up in La Rochelle. He moved there after leaving his native Provence and first trying, unsuccessfully, to adapt to the Aveyron, Bas-Rhin and Loire-Atlantique *départements*. I admired his freedom, in contrast to my inability to move away from my loved ones. I dreaded the silence when I moved in with him. His house was far from all the lively places, and surrounded by a high wooden fence. My mother often repeated that life as a couple was a succession of compromises, so I told myself that this would be the first one.

In Paris, I study people, watch how they walk, scan their faces. The crowd, friendly yesterday, has turned hostile. The danger might be lurking under that hat or behind that umbrella, in that car or on the pavement opposite. I quicken my pace, I refuse to about-turn and capitulate. I don't want to let fear control my life anymore. For too long, I've been shriveled up inside myself. For too long, I've been walking alongside my life. I enter a park, a sign says it's the Square des Batignolles. I sit down on the first bench I come to and wait for my heart to resume its normal rhythm. It's almost there when I feel my phone vibrating in my bag. The screen shows a number I don't recognize. Only my mother, Jeanne, and the agency that employs me have my number, and their numbers are all stored on my phone. I let it ring, waiting for the caller to get my impersonal voicemail. They immediately call again. My heart is racing once more. I stare at the screen, petrified. The ringing stops and, seconds later, more vibrating tells me a message has been left. From the first word, the voice of my caller quells my anxiety. I call him back immediately.

"Clément, it's me."

"How are you doing? You can tell me the truth."

For almost an hour, I tell my brother everything. All that I didn't tell him before so as not to worry him. To protect Jérémy, too. I didn't want anyone thinking badly of him. My brother was one of the only people never to express the slightest doubt about him. I feared his reaction when I left for La Rochelle, but he encouraged me, maybe to distance me from the grief surrounding the death of our father. A thousand times I've wanted to call him. A thousand times I've thought better of it. I was the big sister, the one who stood up for him in the playground, who covered for him when he snuck out, who was terrified when he didn't get back. I knew that he himself wouldn't call. He communicates mainly through private messages on Instagram. I installed the app and signed up just to follow him. Clément is a traveler. When he was little, he would fall asleep gazing at the illuminated globe beside his bed. At eighteen, just after getting his *baccalauréat* at our parents' insistence, he set off to discover the world. Backpack, best friend, and that was it. When he returned a year later, my mother hoped his wanderlust had been satisfied, but he was only just starting. Over the past ten years, I've seen him more often in photos than in the flesh, but his total fulfillment radiates from the screen. On Instagram, more than a hundred thousand followers wait for his videos of northern lights, russet mountains, translucent waters or sandstorms.

"How d'you get my number?"

"Mom."

"Tell her nothing, okay?"

"Promise. She thinks you just need a bit of space, that it'll sort itself out. But don't hang around too long, she needs to know she's a granny before your kid's eighteen!"

I tell him about my bump, which I can still hide thanks to sweatshirts that are three times too big. About my fears for my baby's future. The words come out in rapid-fire, he's the first person I can confide in on the subject, I only just spare him a full medical report on my cervix.

He listens to me patiently, without interrupting, unless it's to laugh or show empathy. Hearing his voice is lovely, but reminds me, painfully, that all my loved ones are far away.

"I'm back in France in three weeks, can I come and see you?"

"You bet!"

"I'll just do a little detour to La Rochelle, there are some teeth I need to knock out."

I laugh, before forbidding him from getting involved.

"I've lost enough people through this whole business, Clément. Leave it to me. I'll sort it out."

"Oh, on the subject, I nearly forgot! I received a message from Mel on Insta. She asked me for your new number. That's why I asked Mom if you'd changed it. Can I give it to her?"

40
JEANNE

Jeanne waited for the letters as much as she dreaded them. For a few minutes they brought Pierre back to life, and consequently, her, too. The downside was the sting of absence when she reached the last word. She could reread them, over and over again, but the magic only worked once.

Today's letter, like the one before, revived a buried memory. The mystery surrounding these letters was total. Who on earth could know about these episodes, so insignificant that Jeanne had forgotten them, and yet so typical of her life with Pierre? Now that it was written down in black and white, she could see it clearly: their love hadn't been about great joy, but rather about a succession of small moments of happiness.

Spring 2012

It's Pierre's last day at work. This evening, after more than forty years teaching English to more or less attentive students, he will be retired. He carried out his profession with passion and rigor, convinced of its usefulness. Jeanne, who has been retired for a few months, knows how depressing the feeling of no longer serving a purpose, along with the boredom, can be. She's delighted her husband will be joining her in her long days with no alarm clock or any imposed routine. To celebrate the occasion, she has organized a surprise. For several weeks, with the help of her sister, who is up on IT and social networks, she has been contacting the pupils who, year after year, have marked her husband's life. Each one agreed to record a video for their former teacher. When watching it, Pierre is moved to tears. Until the end of his life, not a month went by without him rewatching the video, and being reminded of how much love it took to make such a gift.

Jeanne held onto the letter for several minutes so as not to break this bridge to the other side. Once fully back in the present, she put it with the others in the drawer of her bedside table, and then sat down in front of her sewing machine. It was an old manual model, which needed careful handling to avoid snapping the thread or jamming the needle, but Jeanne knew it by heart, and how to talk to it so it gave of its best. When Iris had told her about this woman in a wheelchair, a tiny ember had flickered inside her. She had sent her two lodgers to fetch her gear from the cellar, without revealing her intentions to them. Casually, she had asked Iris about her friend's build. Then she had drawn a pattern. A few minutes had sufficed for the old reflexes to resurface and the skills to return.

For more than forty years, Jeanne had been a *petite main*, or seamstress, at Dior. She had started at twenty years old, thanks to a friend of her mother, who had noticed Jeanne's patience and talent. From being an apprentice, she had climbed the ladder, as the decades went by, to become the atelier's head seamstress. She had loved the tailored styles as much as the floaty or haute couture ones, the pattern-cutting as much as the embroidering or the making up, she had worn out her eyes and fingers, she had stitched, unpicked, restitched and re-unpicked, tested her patience to the limit, but her passion had remained intact. Each garment demanded tens, even hundreds, of hours of team work. Finally seeing the finished item was always a shared thrill. Her retirement had been as much a joy as a sacrifice. She would be able to spend more time with Pierre, but she would miss the very special atmosphere of the atelier. To compensate, she had recreated her own atelier at home, in the second bedroom. Careerwise, Jeanne still had only one regret: not having met Christian Dior, who had died several years before she had started working there.

After about an hour, Jeanne stopped. The sewing was done. She had made three garments, to increase the chance of meeting the needs of the lady they were for. She waited for Iris's return at the end of the day like a kid waits for Santa. It had been a long time since she'd felt such excitement.

"Iris, I've sewn a little something for your friend," she announced, without waiting for the door to close.

She sat the young woman down on the sofa and presented the clothes to her, one by one:

"I went to an association to find out about specific clothing requirements when in a wheelchair. The trousers have an elasticated waist that's higher at the back, better when seated. They have no pockets, which could be uncomfortable. I used a cotton with elastane. For the dress, I put on snap fasteners, but I could replace them with Velcro if it's more practical. The opening can be at the front or the back, and the length is sufficient to cover the legs. The last piece is a cape that slips on over the head. Here again, it can fasten at the front or back, depending on whether it's the lady doing it, or her assistant. I've made it in gabardine, a tight weave that stands up well to rain and cold. I've added a hood with a drawstring. There we are, I don't know if it was a good idea, maybe you'll think I'm not minding my own business, but when you told me about your friend's predicament, I thought I might be able to help her."

Jeanne didn't have to wait for Iris's reaction. Starting with a long sob, she stammered out thanks and praise. Jeanne, not expecting as much, couldn't hold back her tears, and it was this spectacle, gushing with emotion, that Théo had the pleasure of coming home to.

41
THÉO

I'm fond of them, the two old girls, don't get me wrong. But still, if they could quit blubbering at every opportunity, it would give me a break. It's open doors on the tear ducts, and at this rate, we'll all go under. This evening, back from a real pain of day at work, I find them bawling a duet. Like some fountain—I almost toss a coin at them and make a wish. They stop when they see me and start laughing. I've seen some weird people in my life, but they really take the cake.

I say hi from a distance and bolt to my room. At work, I got a call from my mother's place. The nurse left a message, my mother had a pulmonary embolism last night, she's in hospital. I called as soon as I heard the message, and while the phone was ringing, I imagined all sorts. When the nurse told me she was stable, I was relieved, but straight after, disappointed. One day they'll call to tell me she's dead, and I'll be beyond upset, because it will mean never again, no more hope, no more forgiveness, no more Mom, but I'll be happy for her, because she'll be free. Free from her lifeless body, free from this life that she couldn't quite reach. She sometimes told me dribs and drabs about her childhood, and in her place, anyone would have done the same and anesthetized themselves rather than live with such memories.

I'll go and see her when she's back from hospital, in a few days' time according to the nurse.

I scroll around on my phone for a while, watching pointless videos, waiting for time to go by and take my dark mood with it.

Jeanne comes to tell me she's made a Jerusalem-artichoke gratin, and it will be ready in 30 minutes. No idea what that is, and the name hardly inspires confidence, but I'm starving and, I admit, I prefer eating with them than with my phone.

I have time to take a shower. I lay out clean shorts and T-shirt, and go to the bathroom. Iris washes in the morning, Jeanne once we've left, me in the evening. It fell into place naturally. I open the door without noticing that the light is on.

"AAAAAAAAAAAAAAAAAAH!" screams Iris, naked under the shower.

"AAAAAAAAAAAAAAH YOURSELF!" I scream, clocking her rounded tummy.

She pushes me like a domino against the door, which shuts, and the two of us find ourselves together in the tiny room, and I have to look at the ceiling to avoid breasts, ass, or worse, a pregnant woman's belly. Jeanne hammers at the door:

"Is everything okay?"

"Yes, yes," says Iris. "I thought I saw something, but I was mistaken."

"Really convincing," I whisper. "You're pregnant?"

She wraps a towel around her:

"No."

"Oh. Well, I'm sorry to inform you that you have a Quincke's edema of the stomach."

She responds by ejecting me from the bathroom.

I return to my room, thinking the world is full of weird people. When I was small, the psychologists and teachers were determined that I should be like everyone else, despite my situation. As soon as I did something odd, as soon as I stepped out of the box, it seemed crucial to them to get me right back inside it. But the older I get, the more reassured I am. I believe that the norm is, in fact, not being normal.

We sit at the table twenty minutes later. Iris's hair is still moist, and her eyes are, too. Barely seated, she announces that she has something to tell us.

42
Iris

Three pairs of eyes stare at me, intently. For once, it's Boudine's that scare me the least. I've imagined this conversation dozens of times, and it was easier in my head. I suppose it is only the second time I'll be saying it out loud.

"I'm pregnant."

"But . . . how?" Jeanne exclaims.

Théo guffaws:

"Well, you see, the daddy plants the seed in the mummy's tummy, and pushes it right in with his willy."

Jeanne puts down her fork:

"Thank you, young man, I daresay I know more than you do on the subject. Iris, how long have you been pregnant?"

"Nearly six months."

"So you were already, when you came here?"

I nod:

"I'm so sorry, Jeanne. I should have told you on the first day, but I was scared you wouldn't rent the room to me. And after that, I never found the right moment. I thought about doing so very often, but didn't know how to go about it."

Jeanne looks hard at me, without a word. Her expression is inscrutable. She stands up and walks off with her plate, although it's still full.

"Nice one, she took it well," Théo quips, sniggering.

"I'm sorry I lied to you, too."

Sarcasm gives way to surprise. He raises his eyebrows and musters a kind of smile:

"Don't worry. You're not in an easy situation. No hard feelings."

I join Jeanne in the kitchen. She's furiously scrubbing a saucepan. Her back is hunched, it's the first time she looks her age. Boudine has stretched out over her feet.

"I'm truly sorry, Jeanne. I don't like to lie. I didn't really have any choice. I hope you will forgive me."

She takes a deep breath:

"I thought I was over it," she whispers.

"What do you mean?"

She puts down the sponge, dries her hands, and faces me:

"Much as I try, sincerely try, whenever I'm told about a pregnancy, even when it's someone I dearly love, sadness trumps joy."

I remember the cradle in the cellar, the teddy bear, the little clouds on the wallpaper in my room, and I understand.

"You didn't have any . . . "

"No. We tried everything. It's my deepest wound. I thought time would heal it. Don't worry, in a few days all will be fine."

She broke off for a moment, then continued:

"You can stay here for as long as you like, Iris. I won't ask you any questions, but if, one day, you feel like telling me, I'll be here."

She awkwardly wipes away the tears tumbling down her cheeks. I struggle to hold back my own. Théo opens the kitchen door, empty plate in hand:

"I wouldn't mind a bit more of that Jerusalem thingy, there . . . Oh no, you're not both at it again! Never seen anything like it, at this rate, it's incontinence."

Jeanne laughs, before serving him another portion of gratin. It's an ordinary scene, people together in a kitchen, on a week night, and yet, as I observe it, for the first time in ages, I feel good.

43
JEANNE

"The girl's pregnant," Jeanne announced, straight off.

She knew that Pierre was partial to such stories, and was keen to tell him about it. Other people's lives and, more particularly, the surprises in them, was certainly not their favorite topic of conversation, but still came quite high up.

"I reacted badly," she continued. "I soon pulled myself together, but all the same, the poor girl, she must have felt bad."

Jeanne still vividly remembered the announcement of her colleague Maryse's pregnancy. The two of them were close, their friendship having blossomed over the years, and yet Jeanne had been the only one not to congratulate her warmly. While everyone was hugging Maryse and wishing her the best, Jeanne had feigned a sudden ailment and rushed off, reappearing only three days later, once the euphoria had subsided—and her grief, too. Guilt made the whole thing even more difficult. She reproached herself for being unable to rejoice sincerely in others' happiness. She couldn't help it. Her unhappiness took up all the space. Others had what she couldn't manage to have.

Jeanne's desire for a child had overshadowed her entire life. As a little girl, her mother had given her a porcelain doll whom she had named Claudine, and would change, feed, and cradle as if it were a real baby.

Her adolescence had been one of constant impatience. She would read fairy tales thinking that, one day, she'd be among those who "got married, had many children, and lived happily ever after."

Meeting Pierre had turned her desire into a plan. For

fifteen years, they had done everything possible to create a life. They had listened to the many pieces of advice given to them: try thinking about it less, relax, only make love at certain times, or in certain positions, favor certain foods over others. They had consulted specialists, general practitioners, hypnotizers, priests, had experienced hope so often, followed by unfathomable disappointment, had been united, divided, become distant, closer, had counted cycles, days, capsules, symptoms, sheep. They had decorated and furnished their third room. Jeanne had envied, dreadfully, excessively, those who saw their stomachs expanding while hers remained hopelessly flat.

Inevitably, the clock had chimed "too late." No more hope, no more plans, but an infinity of regrets. Crying over what had never been and no longer would be. The void left by vanished hope had to be filled. She must find other sources of fulfillment, of joy, create a different kind of family to that planned, and try to think as little as possible about what life would have been, if.

The lack of a child had been the cornerstone of Jeanne's existence.

"I thought I'd gotten over it, my love. But, since you're no longer here, I have to bear that absence alone."

It had taken Jeanne time to understand her sister, Louise, who hadn't wanted to be a mother. Their parents, aunts, teachers, friends, everyone had tried to reason with her, considering her decision to be an aberration. Jeanne's thinking had evolved since then. She was well placed to know that women didn't have a vocation to give birth, and that the pressure they endured on the subject was stifling. How often had she and Louise had to respond to the question, "so, when's that baby coming?", each sister having her own reason to find it insufferable.

So as not to leave Pierre on a downer, Jeanne went on to tell him about the apron she had started to make, and her renewed pleasure in sewing. And then told him about the delicious *Paris-Brest* pastry the young man had had them try.

As she was leaving, after first greeting Simone, who was busy chatting with a newcomer, Jeanne realized that, for the first time, she hadn't needed notes to find things to talk about.

44
THÉO

Whenever I'm back in my mother's room, I put music on for her. When she ended up here, I was allowed to bring her player and CDs. She'd loved listening to music, there was always some on. She'd pick discs according to her mood. When I'd get home from school, I'd listen out to know what state I'd find her in. If it was Barry White, ABBA or Marvin Gaye, she'd be cheerful, the house would be tidy, she'd dance, sing and hug me tight, calling me "baby." If it was Nina Simone, Joni Mitchell, or Ella Fitzgerald, she'd be sitting at the table, staring into space, cheeks streaked black with mascara, a bottle or two in front of her.

I only brought cheery albums, she's cried enough for a lifetime. And anyhow, I don't know if she listens, or even hears. In the end, I think it's for myself that I put the music on. It's like a link between us, something that's like before.

A nurse enters the room and hums the Barry White song. She explains to me that the blood clot from the embolism has been resorbed, my mother is undergoing treatment, and all should be fine. I gaze at the body lying on the bed, eyelids closed, bloodless lips, and think that, sometimes, it'd be better if all wasn't fine.

"I have to give her a wash, you want to stay?"

There's a limit. I'm prepared to do quite a few things, but not that. I take the chance to go out and have a cig. I never smoke as much as when I visit my mother. I'm not the only one, there are two others on the terrace. I recognize them, family of patients. Here, you're holding your breath. If you don't grab some fresh air, you won't last.

When I return to the room, my mother is in the armchair and the CD has stopped. I put on ABBA and sit in front of her. I've stuck a text and some photos on the wall. I'm the only person to visit her. All of her friends have hung back in her old life. There are snaps of her, lots, a few of me, and two of her other son. He's very little in them, I couldn't find any more recent ones. His father has sole custody of him. I barely knew him. I was nearly eight when my mother announced to me that I was going to have a brother. I was at the kids' home. I blubbered for days, I was furious, I even smashed in that schmuck Johann's face when, for once, he'd done nothing. I couldn't understand why she'd want another child when she could have me, but wouldn't take me home. She did get me back a while later, the law allowed it because she wasn't drinking anymore and lived in a house with her guy and their baby. He was six months old. I tried not to love him, tried to hold against him his taking what belonged to me, but I didn't succeed. He'd chuckle as soon as I said a word, he followed me everywhere, and could say my name before saying daddy or mommy. We slept in the same room, the four of us sat around the table to eat, it was a family, or it sure seemed like it, at any rate, from the inside. Marc, her guy, was cool, he got me to do my homework and took me to football matches. It was the first time I had a father since mine had died, just after my birth. In short, perfect family life lasted a year. My mother went back to drinking. Marc waited a few months, and finally left when he realized that no one could compete with a bottle. He said he'd find out about taking me with him, but I didn't want to abandon my mother. After that, social services sent me back to the kids' home. Marc and my brother came to see me several times, and then one day they moved house, the letters became less frequent, I stopped opening them, end of story.

When I get back to the apartment, I'm in a Nina Simone mood. Iris and Jeanne are in the sitting room, I rush to my room without greeting them. My belly aches and I need to lie down. But before I've even taken off my coat, there's knocking on the door. It's Iris, suggesting I join them for a game of Scrabble:

"No thanks, I don't feel like it."

"Go on, come! I'm just getting thrashed, it'd be good to start from scratch."

"I told you I don't feel like it."

"Too bad, no dessert for you," she says, laughing.

"You can keep your damn dessert. Leave me alone."

"Okay, try being polite. I was joking."

I should leave it there. I know it. It's not her I'm angry with. But it's her who's in front of me.

"I don't need lessons from a broad who's having a kid without a father."

Her face reddens:

"Who do you think you are to judge me? WHO DO YOU THINK YOU ARE?"

"Don't get your panties in a bunch."

"Wow! That's your level of debate? I bow down, you're too good."

Jeanne must have heard the shouting, she turns up, seeming concerned. She looks first at one of us, then at the other, moves towards me and, before I have time to defend myself, takes me in her arms.

45
Iris

We arranged to meet at a café. I get there first, sit at a table, and scroll through Instagram to make time pass quicker. My brother is in Patagonia. The landscapes are magnificent and the locals seem welcoming, but, despite Clément's many experiences, I've never caught the travel bug. I've enjoyed the rare trips I've been on, but was always pleased to get my bearings back. I'm a neutered cat: I never stray too far from my sofa.

"Hi, Iris."

Mel sits down opposite me. Instantly, all my anxiety at the thought of this meeting melts away. She'd sent me a message the day after my brother's call, to suggest we talk. Knowing her so well, I can imagine how pleased she is to see me again, despite her mask of detachment.

"I'm so sorry, Mel."

"Me too. I should have understood."

"I hadn't understood, myself."

"You know he rang me?"

My heart stops.

"Supposedly, to ask my advice on some legal matter," she adds. "He carefully avoided telling me that you'd left. He's got a cheek, two years without a peep, and then he just appears, like Bernadette at the grotto. Asshole."

She frowns:

"Can I call him an asshole now?"

I laugh:

"It's almost too nice."

"I missed you."

"I missed you, too."

We stay there for two hours, which feels like ten minutes. Our closeness returns as if never dented. The friendship picks up from where we left it. Mel tells me about the legal practice she works in, about cases she's defending, about Loïc, about their one-bed apartment in the 6th arrondissement, about Marie and Gaëlle, about her parents, about before. And she wants to know everything about my departure and my relationship with Jérémy.

"You know he's going to keep looking for you?" she asks me, before leaving.

"I know."

"I've been doing aikido for six months, I can easily make him bite his own balls off."

"If he had any, people would know about it."

She bursts out laughing.

"You should lodge a complaint against that bastard, Iris, ask for a protection order."

"It might all settle down. He'll end up moving on to something else. He has no reason to think I'm in Paris. I chose the most populated city, I'm a needle in a haystack."

She finally gives up, but not without first letting out a string of insults. It's her way of releasing stress, like a fart, but better. Before going, she walks around the table and gives me a hug. I've not told her about the life growing inside me. I was keeping the best till last.

"What the hell is that?" she cries, looking at my belly.

"Don't know, it sprang up last night."

"OMG! I'm going to be an auntie!"

She hugs me again, and congratulates me again and again, before declaring that my kid had better be less dumb than his father.

Returning to the apartment, I feel like I'm emerging from prolonged hibernation. I'm back in touch with my life, having lost sight of it. Solitude had become my sole companion. By getting Mel back, I'm getting myself back.

I climb the stairs with the firm intention of polishing off that coffee éclair Theo brought me last night, to apologize for his reaction. I was going to park him in the stupid-little-bastards category, until he explained that he'd had a very difficult day. He didn't say more, he didn't need to. Sometimes there's the darkness in his eyes of those who've faced the depths of it.

I'm almost at the third floor when ringing from my bag tells me I've a new message. Convinced I'll find a word from Mel, I automatically grab my phone and almost drop it on the floor when I recognize the number displayed.

"My angel, where are you?"

He's found out my number.

46
JEANNE

Jeanne was leaving for the cemetery when Victor stopped her:

"Madame Perrin, could you come here for a moment, please?"

She checked her watch, anxiously: the bus was always punctual, and she had to be, too, if she didn't want her time with Pierre curtailed.

"It won't take long," the caretaker reassured her.

She followed him into his apartment, on the ground floor, facing the courtyard. Boudine sniffed every corner of it, as usual. Victor would deliberately leave dry food around the place for his cat, which was blind and paralyzed in its back legs. The poor creature was still alive thanks only to several operations, and medication that could get a heartbeat out of a chair. Victor recognized his own obsession with saving it, but had a worthy explanation: he had found the Siamese cat lying on his doormat four years earlier, when he'd returned from the hospital where his beloved mother had just passed. He was about to shoo it away when he noticed its squint. Just like his mother's. That was all he had needed to tweak his Catholic faith and convince himself that his mother was now short-haired.

"It's about the young lady who lives with you."

"Iris?" Jeanne asked, surprised.

The man nodded and his smile left little doubt as to the direction of the conversation.

"I'd like to apologize for her fall in the stairs. If I hadn't polished the steps, it wouldn't have happened."

"I think she's forgotten about it. I really must go, Victor."

"Do you think she likes flowers?"

Jeanne relaxed and gave the caretaker's shoulder an affectionate squeeze:

"I think that, above all, she's going through a tricky period. Flowers would certainly please her, but don't expect anything back."

Victor smiled:

"Okay, I understand."

He walked Jeanne to the building's entrance, and before she made for the bus stop, asked her if chocolates might please Iris more.

Jeanne had to run for the bus. The doors were closing when she dived inside. It took several long minutes for her to get her breath back, and yet no one thought of offering her a seat. She didn't care: she'd soon be with Pierre.

Simone was on the bench when Jeanne arrived, but she wasn't alone. Beside her, and clearly deep in conversation with her, was a bearded man. Jeanne's distance vision was no longer what it was, but it seemed to her that it was the very person Simone had been chatting to a few days earlier. She went over to greet them.

"Jeanne, let me introduce you to Richard," Simone said, solemnly. "Richard is the widower of Mathilde, who rests in the large vault at the end of the path."

Then, turning to Richard:

"I spoke to you of Jeanne, the widow of Pierre."

Jeanne didn't know how to respond to this introduction, which reminded her of the school gates of her childhood, when the adults didn't have a name but were "the mom of" or "the dad of." She inclined her head politely, then joined her husband, delighted to have two juicy anecdotes to tell him.

47
THÉO

I've been shut away in my room for ten minutes, not daring to come out. A little out of fear, a lot out of shame.

For several days, Iris had been asking me to show her how to make a pear-and-chocolate charlotte. So I brought all the gear home earlier and suggested we hit the kitchen. Iris was happy, Jeanne was happy, Boudine was happy, I was happy—pear-and-chocolate charlottes must be the solution to world peace.

I got Iris to peel the pears, and told Jeanne she'd be soaking the ladyfingers, which made her laugh, no idea why. I was about to start on the mousse when the drama in three acts unfolded.

Iris said "I've cut myself."

Jeanne said "It's deep."

I said "bye-bye."

I shot off to my room without looking—for all I know, her finger might be lost among the ladyfingers.

I can't help it, I've always had a blood phobia. There's no warning: if I see a drop, my body shuts down. When I was little, I often had nosebleeds, and every time I'd see stars, and then straight after I'd see the floor in close-up. Generally, anything related to the inside of the body makes me terribly anxious. Once, a psychologist tried to teach me deep breathing to calm me down. Much as I told him it would do the opposite, he insisted that I focus on the air entering my throat, and into my lungs. He was less smug when I dived headfirst into his shagpile rug. Similarly, I never could play that Operation game, or watch *Once Upon a Time . . . Life*.

At middle school, we had to do the "PSC1." Once I realized

that this was first-aid training, I said no thanks, but then I thought of my mother. Maybe if someone had given her a cardiac massage on the day of her accident, her brain wouldn't have lacked oxygen for so long. So I went to the training, and saw it all: bleeding, cardiac arrest, stroke, burns, open wounds, they spared me nothing. I kept my eyes closed more often than open, but I got my certificate.

I open my bedroom door. Not a sound. I call out to Jeanne, no reply. I slip out into the corridor and open the bathroom door. A bottle of disinfectant and a box of dressings are there on the washbasin. I call out to Iris, to Boudine, no reaction. I'm starting to freak out. Maybe it was really serious and they went off to the hospital, and I'd just left them in the lurch. I cross the sitting room to go and check in the kitchen. I just catch them whispering before opening the door. Thank goodness, or they'd have had me. I don't think I'll ever forget the scene. Iris and Jeanne lying on the floor, eyes closed, daubed in ketchup. Boudine's tongue not missing a drop of it. They're trying not to laugh, but I can see their stomachs twitching. It's the pits. I'm starting to really dig these two.

48
Iris

Nadia is wearing the dress Jeanne made for her. It suits her perfectly and looks straight off a designer's catwalk. On the day I brought her the clothes, awkwardness prevailed. She kept insisting on paying Jeanne, or at the very least, paying for the fabric, but, over the phone, my roommate wouldn't hear of it, accepting only Nadia's thanks. In desperation, Nadia slipped a few cakes she'd made that morning into my bag, and I could see by her expression that, if I didn't want to end up, inadvertently, under her wheels, I shouldn't argue.

"My cape caused a sensation in the group," she tells me, smiling broadly.

"The group?"

"My MS support group. I've never mentioned it to you? I've been going since my diagnosis, it allows me to talk with people who know what I'm on about. It does me so much good, even if it can, sometimes, be difficult. Anyway, everyone loved the cape. One can find them in a few specialist shops, but never as stylish!"

She reaches out for a glass on the table but immediately lets her arm fall, grimacing.

"Are you in pain?"

"My neck's stiff, I must have slept in an awkward position."

"Would you like me to try to ease it?"

"You know how to?"

I help her to lie on her bed, and let my hands find their way again, having lost it for months. I gently mobilize her muscles into an unpainful position, turn her head to the right, to the left, and as the minutes pass, I can feel the contraction easing.

"Torticollis is like a really bad cramp," I explain, massaging her trapezius muscles. "The Jones technique is ideal to ease the pain and restore mobility."

Nadia looks up at me:

"Iris, how do you know all this?"

"I studied physical therapy."

"And why aren't you practicing?"

To avoid answering, I help her to get up. She turns her head carefully and seems to have regained range.

"It's still a bit sensitive, but much less than before! My washbasin is leaking, can you do plumbing, too?"

"Of course! I can also do your hair, but no complaints if you look like a plowed field."

She laughs, but has the tact not to go any further. Nadia once told me that she knew I was one of her own. I didn't immediately get what she meant, but later, thanks to a chat about her past, she was more specific: "There's an invisible tie between women who have suffered. We recognize each other."

She won't try to take what I don't want to give her. One day, perhaps, I'll open up to this woman, to whom I'm becoming increasingly attached.

The door flies open and Nadia's son bounds in, schoolbag on back. He throws everything off, comes to kiss his mother, then looks at me as if seeing me for the first time:

"Have you got a baby in your tummy?"

"No, just some chocolate."

His mother's eyes land at the level of my navel. She stares wide-eyed, and puts her hand to her mouth:

"Well blow me! I didn't notice a thing!"

I don't deny it, I can't deny it anymore. My bump is so big, I could house the Kardashians inside it.

"Are you married?" Léo asks me.

Nadia explains to him that one mustn't ask questions like that to strangers, he replies that I'm not a stranger, and my mind wanders far away from the conversation and down into an inside pocket of my bag, and into my phone, where dozens of messages from Jérémy are piling up.

49
JEANNE

Jeanne closed her eyes and breathed in the aroma from a branch of fir. It had the power to transport her back to her childhood. She had always adored Christmas. From the first day of Advent, she and her sister Louise thought of just one thing: the Christmas Eve *réveillon*. This meant a reunion of the whole family in their Aunt Adélaïde's large house. To allay her impatience, Jeanne would decorate the walls and furniture with garlands and silver stars, which she'd make out of chocolate-bar wrappers, collected for that purpose over the year. On the big night itself, there were about twenty of them gathered around the big fir tree. The women would prepare the dinner to a chorus of laughter, the men would take charge of lighting the fire or cutting branches of holly to adorn the table, while Jeanne and her cousins would set up the crèche and position the figurines. After the guinea-fowl, Yule log, and chocolate truffles, everyone would wrap up and head off to midnight Mass. Jeanne had fond memories of the nights that would follow. The seven cousins shared two beds, as best they could, and promised their parents to sleep—which they never could, so busy were they trying to catch Father Christmas in action. They would be up at the crack of dawn to find out what present had been left beside their shoes. One year, Jeanne had received a doll whose eyelids closed when lying down. She still had it, sitting on top of the wardrobe in her bedroom. She appreciated her presents all the more because, having never really believed that Father Christmas story, she knew the sacrifice they meant for her parents. Those noisy, joyful Christmases contrasted painfully with the silence she now knew. Happily, this evening, the solitude of two others had joined her own.

"Where do I put the holly?" asked Théo.

Jeanne seized the branch and placed it at the center of the table.

It was the first Christmas without Pierre. He loved this celebration as much as her, and contrary to what she had once feared, the absence of a child hadn't spoilt their enjoyment one bit. Together, they would stroll the streets of Paris, noses in the air, to admire the festive lights. Christmas Eve was the chance to put together a great dinner and treat themselves. It was a real challenge to keep coming up with ideas for presents after several decades of living together, but Jeanne and Pierre were determined to meet it. The satisfaction of surprising their beloved, seeing their eyes sparkle, couldn't be beaten.

Jeanne took a gulp of champagne to dissolve the painful lump now in her throat, and went to sit at the table. Iris and Théo had insisted on preparing everything themselves, she'd barely been allowed into the sitting room. This hadn't been easy for her.

"Who opened the oysters?" she asked, before picking bits of shell off her tongue.

"I'd never done it before, bro!" Théo said, defensively.

"*Bro?*" Jeanne spluttered.

"Sorry, it's just an expression, I call everyone that. But I still don't know how you can eat those things, even Boudin won't touch them, and she eats my dirty socks."

The main course was greeted with fewer reservations. The capon was tender and the chestnuts well-seasoned.

"It's not even ten o'clock," Jeanne pointed out, when they had finished the dish. "A *réveillon* worthy of the name doesn't finish before midnight. How about we delay dessert by playing a game?"

"Terrific," said Théo, rolling his eyes. "We couldn't just jump out of the window instead?"

"It's lovely you're so enthusiastic," said Iris. "It must be the magic of Christmas."

Théo took advantage of Jeanne's absence, while she was looking for a game in the hall sideboard, to give Iris the finger. She smiled innocently back at him. Jeanne returned with a round, green-baize lined tray, and five dice:

"Let's play Yahtzee!" she suggested.

For the first two rounds, Théo beat his opponents hands down, and declared that, in the end, he liked this game a lot. His luck finally turned, and he had loss after loss. Midnight was approaching when Jeanne rolled the dice for the last time. Five identical sides appeared.

"Yahtzee!" she cried, arms in the air. "I've won!"

"I'm well PO'd," muttered Théo.

Jeanne thought she'd misheard:

"You're what?"

"PO'd. That I've been KO'd."

"Good grief, and I think I'm having a CVA. I can't understand a word you're saying."

Iris bursts out laughing:

"It means he's outraged he lost."

"I didn't lose, I came second. It's you who lost."

"If you carry on, it's my waters I'm going to lose."

Théo and Jeanne guffaw at this overkill from Iris, who diverts the attention by taking two wrapped gifts from a bag hanging on her chair. She hands them one each:

"It's not much, but Merry Christmas!"

Théo got a poster depicting all the patisserie classics, and Jeanne a little pincushion. They both thanked her, and then Jeanne scurried off to her room and returned with two presents.

"Wow!" murmured Iris, clearly touched, as she unfolded a long black dress.

Jeanne explained that it was empire-line, perfect for accommodating her bump until the end of her pregnancy. As for Théo, he was given a khaki sweatshirt and an apron. He thanked the two women and shook his head:

"I haven't got anything for you two, really sorry. I'm not used to giving Christmas presents, or receiving them. But let's just say I'm giving you the Yule log I made."

Jeanne shook her head with a disapproving look.

"You're right to be sorry, bro, I'm well PO'd."

50
THÉO

It's crazy how many people celebrate the start of a new year as if it were some kind of deliverance, who really think it's going to change the direction of things. My mother always took advantage of New Year's Eve to get totally plastered, just to make hay before making her resolutions, which she never kept. At the kids' home, everyone loved seeing in the New Year, a party was organized, it was the event of the month, seeing as no one liked Christmas. I would play it cool, convinced that I really was, so I don't get why it bugs me so much having no one to celebrate it with tonight.

I'm sprawled on my bed, watching some TV series on my phone. There's a timid knock on the door. It must be Jeanne, Iris is partying at a friend's place.

"I've prepared some coquilles Saint-Jacques and opened a good bottle of white, will you join me?"

She's put on an evening dress and some make-up. She looks beautiful.

"I'm in my sweats."

"Stay as you are. I'll give you a little accessory that will make all the difference."

Five minutes later, I sit at the table in sweatpants and a T-shirt, but with a black bow tie around my neck.

It's the first time we're just the two of us. I'm not sure what I can really say of interest to an old lady. But anyhow, she talks for two, which probably means she feels as awkward as I do. She tells me about New Year's Eves spent with her husband, they liked going to places with plenty of people around, restaurants, dances, whatever, as long as there were lots of them to shout

"Happy New Year!" at midnight. It seems like she misses all that; sometimes, she stares into space as if searching for the past there.

I'm fond of her. I sense it wouldn't take much for her to matter to me. She's done nothing to encourage that, hasn't sought to be loved, she's just herself, and that's rare. She pours herself another drink, her third, I can't help counting.

"Another one for you?"

"No thanks."

I always stop before I'm sloshed. I tried it once and loved it. That scared me.

"We had a little ritual, me and my husband," says Jeanne. "Every December 31, we'd jot down on a bit of paper the positive events of the past year, and drop the list into a jar in our bedroom. Next, on another bit of paper, we'd jot down all the negative events, those we wanted to leave in the past, and then burn the list. How about we do that together?"

I don't really have a view on this, the idea doesn't bother me, but doesn't make me want to jump for joy either, let's just say I can take it or leave it, so I say O.K..

While we write down the positive things, we tell each other a few of them. My job and finding this apartment are my two best things. Leaving the kids' home, too, even if that's a bit on the negative list, too. Jeanne tells me about a stay in Alsace early in the year, and the weeks when her husband was still here.

While we write down the negative things, on the other hand, we don't share anything. I feel like I'm at school, I put my arm over the paper so Jeanne can't copy, and see her doing the same. When we're done, we fold up the lists and burn them in the sink. Jeanne tries to hide her tears, wiping them away before they even well up. I pretend not to notice, but feel sorry for her so give her a little tap on the shoulder. From the way she reels, I think I underestimated my strength.

"I didn't tell you, Théo, but on my list of positive events, I wrote your name and Iris's. I found it hard to get used to at first, but I'm really happy you're both here. You're a nice boy."

And at that, don't know why, but I start blubbering like a kid. Jeanne takes me in her arms, and it's as if she's putting coins into the tear machine, they stream and stream like they're never going to stop. And that's exactly why I never allow myself to start.

I tell her everything. My mother, the drinking, the kids' home, Manon, my father dying, my mother's baby, the car accident. She says nothing, just hands me tissues and strokes my cheek, but I sense she understands me. *Really* understands me. It does me so much good. It's very strange, as if it's all become less heavy, now that she's carrying it with me.

At midnight, we watch the countdown on TV, and wish each other a happy new year at the same time as the presenters, Nikos Aliagas and Arthur, do. We go off to bed shortly after, and there's a message waiting for me on my phone.

"Happy New Year, Théo! I wish you all the best—good health, money, and especially love. Leïla"

51
Iris

I hesitated over accepting Mel's invitation for New Year's Eve. I decided to go once I realized that my main obstacle was fear. I knew there would be lots of people there, and I wouldn't know any of them. Mustn't let others become a threat. That's what I've been repeating to myself for hours, but the moment I'm about to ring the doorbell, my courage leaves me.

I don't even have time to put my finger on the bell before the door opens and two unidentified bodies jump on me and burst my eardrums. I wasn't expecting to see them. Marie and Gaëlle, my other oldest friends, wrap their four arms around me and hug me tight.

"I didn't miss you at all," says Gaëlle.

"I'm not at all happy to see you," adds Marie.

Mel joins us with all the gentleness of a prop in a rugby scrum. My joy trounces my fear.

There are lots of people around, but we're in our own world. We cover two years in two hours, talking fast, laughing loudly, touching each other, watching each other, as if to make sure that we're really there, together, like before.

"What are you going to call him?" Marie asks me.

"I've a few ideas, but haven't decided yet."

"You'll need to choose his godmother," Gaëlle says, beaming. "Don't forget that my daughter is your goddaughter, if you see what I mean."

I raise my eyebrows:

"No, I don't see? Are you thinking of Mel or Marie?"

"Poor child," she says, sighing. "Not yet born and already abused."

Marie leans closer to me:

"Are you going to tell him?"

My three friends study my reaction. Just like whenever I think of it, I get palpitations.

"He already knows."

"And what if he asks for custody? Or shared custody?" queries Mel.

"I don't think he will."

"Just to bug you, he will," Gaëlle snaps back.

My joy has gone, eclipsed by anxiety. The girls notice and start competing to be the first to make me laugh. It's Marie, with her almost-impression of Shakira, who wins.

Some friends of Mel and Loïc join us. One of them keeps staring at me. It's embarrassing. I feel like asking him if he wants me rare or medium rare.

"Would you like to dance?" he asks, after several minutes of scrutiny.

"No thanks, I dance like a tree trunk."

He laughs. I relax. Talking commits one to nothing. Others aren't a threat.

"You're a friend of Mel's?"

"Yes, a childhood friend. And you?"

"I work at the same practice as Loïc. Are you a lawyer, too?"

"No, a care worker."

It's barely noticeable, but my hypervigilance picks up the shift in attitude. He comes up with a bit more small talk, before telling me that he's just off to find a glass.

"I can't stand him," Mel whispers as she passes behind me. "He's a pig, his brain's in his dick. It's Loïc who insisted on inviting him."

"Don't you worry, I only talked to him to be polite. I'd rather have a fanny grafted onto my forehead than couple up."

"It's almost midnight!" Loïc shouts.

All the voices become one for the countdown. I think back over the past year, wanting to keep only the best. I have to search for it, cling to any rays of sunlight when shadows were gaining ground. Kick my feet harder so as not to drown, and appreciate every gulp of air at the surface. In the end, I'm going to keep the worst, too. As an enhancer of the best, as a negative image of the lovely. Because he was there, too, this past year, oh yes. Behind my navel, basically, in the tomorrows he promised, in the smiles that didn't fade, silently present. This coming year, I'm going to appreciate the air at the surface, see the light among the shadows, laugh behind the tears, find the lovely even when it's well hidden. I wish myself life and its spice.

HAPPY NEW YEAR!

One minute past midnight.

New text message.

"We're there, our big year. Can't wait to be your husband. Wishing you a happy one, my angel."

January

52
JEANNE

Jeanne took as much pleasure as ever in abiding by all the rules of etiquette that went with a new year. She wrote her good wishes on cards kindly supplied by one of the charities to which she gave a small monthly donation, and sent them to a list of people that hadn't changed for years: her cousin Suzanne, her cousin Jacques, her doctor, the oncologist who had treated her, her friend Maryse who had moved to the South, her cousins' children, her former colleagues. She stopped at Victor's to slip him his seasonal gift, turning down the coffee he offered her: she was determined to wish her sister a happy new year before returning to Pierre.

She always dreaded visiting her sister. For a long time, she had managed to avoid doing so. She no longer had any excuse.

Louise was buried two avenues away from Pierre's grave. She had been there for five years, and yet Jeanne couldn't come to terms with it. When Jeanne had fallen ill, her sister, along with Pierre, had been her main support. With their mother and aunt both having died from breast cancer, the two sisters were closely monitored. Jeanne was in remission when Louise felt a lump in her armpit. The end came lightning-fast.

Jeanne had gone through life never feeling the need to make new friends. Her husband and sister sufficed for her to be happy. She appreciated the company of her colleagues, some had even become close, and she liked meeting new people, getting to know those she saw often, the storekeepers, the neighbors, but her nucleus was Pierre and Louise.

Jeanne was two years old when Louise had entered her life. She had soon become her other half, indispensable to her. They were inseparable. The younger sister had followed the elder to Paris when she had got her seamstress job. Louise had found herself a position on the haberdashery counter at the Bon Marché. The garret they then shared had never seemed small to them. It was a cocoon, a nest in which they were happy to find each other in the evening, to laugh and tell each other everything. Meeting Pierre and Roger had in no way diminished their bond.

There are certain presences that can be taken for granted, certain beings who walk so close to you, for such a long time, that they become an extension of yourself. Louise wasn't so much a member of Jeanne's family, as one of Jeanne's own members, like her arms or legs. To live, Jeanne had oxygen, blood, and a little sister. Never would she have imagined that, one day, Louise could be removed from her life.

Jeanne placed the pot of heather at the foot of the stele. Louise's name was just beneath her beloved Roger's.

"Hello, my dear sister," she murmured.

As she left to join Pierre, Jeanne had a sudden chilling thought. She now spent more time with the dead than the living.

Simone was on her bench, without her new friend.

"Happy New Year!" she called out to Jeanne, who stopped when she reached her.

"Thanks, Simone. I wish you a lovely year, good health above all, and love if you fancy it . . . "

She instantly regretted that last bit, but Simone burst into resounding laughter:

"I like to be courted every now and then, but it will never go any further. It's too late for me. I'm eighty-two years old, and I've been living my love here for fifteen years. On the subject, if you don't mind me wishing you something . . . "

She broke off, smiling awkwardly.

"Yes?" queried Jeanne.

"You may think me tactless, but I'd have liked someone to tell me this when there was still time to change things. And anyhow, it's the moment for wishes, isn't it? So, I wish you not to come here every day anymore. Cemeteries are for the dead. Life is to be found on the other side of that gate."

53
Théo

Going back to karate after two weeks of festivities is torture. My stomach's still digesting, and all my brain can focus on is the best-apprentice competition in three days' time. I can't concentrate on what the instructor's saying, I do everything wrong, and that amuses young Sam. Seemingly, his respect went the same way as the Yule log. I lay it on even thicker, making a meal of every move, which is more my style than moving around a tatami mat. My mother used to say that it wasn't a fairy godmother that had leant over my cradle, but a clown. The worse she got, the more I acted the fool. Most of the time, she'd end up laughing; when she refused to laugh, things were really bad.

"Fifty press-ups!" shouts the instructor.

I think he's looking at us, but since he's squint-eyed, I turn around just to be sure. There's no one behind us. He's punishing us for messing around during his class. Sam lies on his front and starts doing the press-ups. I try ignoring the instructor as if not involved, maybe he'll move on to something else.

He comes up to me with a look usually seen on programs about serial killers. I want my legs to take me far away from here, but they seem to have watched the same programs. He stops a few steps away from me:

"It's just risen to a hundred."

I have no choice.

Sam has already finished when I start. He encourages me, but after thirty press-ups, my arms are saying ciao, thanks for everything, it was nice but we'd rather go on without you. I have the physical fitness of a moped.

The instructor congratulates me, I'm not sure if he's taking the piss or means it. Sam winks at me:

"Really sorry, if I'd known you had sponge arms, I wouldn't have laughed so loud."

"Little creep."

He creases up again, but this time silently.

At the end of the class, the instructor comes over to explain to me that martial arts are not to be taken lightly, that they're not merely a sport, but a way of life, that respect is a mainstay, and the lessons make one grow up.

Everyone has gone when I come out. It's cold, I can't feel my arms anymore, but there's something I must do before going home. Just a small detour.

On the way, I think about the competition. I've not slept for several nights now. Philippe's putting pressure on me, I sense that if I'm not selected, he'll take it badly. I found out that he himself had entered the competition for best craftsperson in France years ago, but hadn't gotten through. Nathalie is piling it on, too, telling all the customers about it, sweet-talking me as if I were a chihuahua. And then there's Leïla. I'm afraid of disappointing her. I can see in her eyes that she believes in me. I was already nervous before, now I'm petrified.

I reach Rue Condorcet. A motorbike is parked where I used to sleep in my car. God only knows how many nights I spent here. I stop for a few moments, then turn back. The house with blue shutters is still there.

54
Iris

I hadn't been kissed that passionately for a long time. I don't know how it got to this, it's too dark to make out his features, I don't know his name, but the first thing I sense is his breath on my mouth. His hot lips against mine. Insistently. His tongue licking my mouth. My nose. My chin. My eyes.

"Chrissake, Boudine!"

Straddling my head, the dog drags me out of a weird dream by cleaning my face. When I moved here three months ago, I hoped to get used to her, but I wasn't asking for all this. I've become her best friend. She follows me everywhere, and looks at me the way many would like to be looked at, eyes full of unconditional love, almost imploring. It doesn't bother me, even if, sometimes, in a certain place, I'd prefer to be alone with my roll of toilet paper.

I can't have closed the door properly when I went to bed. I'd have liked to sleep a bit longer. I've just entered the final trimester of my pregnancy, and my sleep gets lighter as my belly gets heavier. Until now, I've been spared the trials many pregnant women go through. My body was clearly saving itself for a final flourish. I've got the lot: acid reflux, swollen and restless legs, hyperactive bladder, sciatica, appearance of stretch marks and disappearance of perineum.

"Want to go for a walk?"

Boudine wags her tail, I take that as a yes. Jeanne had an appointment early this morning, she can't have had time to take her out.

As usual when I go down these damned stairs, I cling to the handrail so as not to do another Surya Bonaly skating move.

I'm carrying Boudine in my free arm—the steps are higher than her, so she'd end up falling like a domino if I didn't. As I reach the ground floor, my face has been licked perfectly clean.

We stay in the neighborhood. I'm getting to know my way around here. I turned up with zero feelings for the place, and now its noises, smells, facades have become familiar to me. I always thought I was resistant to change, always thought "home" was where all my memories were, what I was used to. I'm realizing, through living it, that "home" is wherever I am. In this neighborhood, this street, this building, this apartment, this bedroom, which were all unknown to me, I have found a home.

Guided by my stomach, I enter Théo's bakery. A young woman is serving a customer, then it's my turn.

"Morning, a *chocolatine*, please."

She looks at me as if I'd insulted her. I've already observed, frequently, the effect this word has on people who don't live in the South-West.

"We don't do those here," she says, with a little smirk. "But I'd recommend a *pain au chocolat*, much nicer."

Picking up on her humor, I play the game:

"A *pain au chocolat*? Is that bread with chocolate inside it? No, really, I'd prefer a *chocolatine*, you have some fine ones here."

"Otherwise, you could have a '*raisintine*,'" she counters, showing me a *pain au raisins*.

Théo, who must have recognized my voice, sticks his head out from the back room:

"Leïla, this woman isn't from around here. Next, she's going to ask you to pop it into a *poche* instead of a *sac*."

I return home with my *chocolatine* in a *poche*. The caretaker is busy cleaning the windows.

"Ah, good morning!" he says. "I haven't seen you yet this year, I wanted to wish you all the best. Good health, work, love, happiness, all that stuff!"

"Thanks very much, Victor, all the best to you, too."

He stares at me, smiling, as if frozen in front of the door. My stomach is crying out.

"Excuse me, I'd like to go through."

He moves over, blushing.

"By the way," he adds, just as I'm going inside, "your name isn't on the mailbox. The postman left a letter addressed to Iris Duhin, is that you?"

It's my turn to freeze. No one has my new address. I pick up my pay slips at the agency, and I've had my mail forwarded to my mother's.

Victor disappears into his apartment and comes back out seconds later with a box of chocolates and an envelope.

"It's no big deal," he stammers, handing them to me, "but I wanted to give you a little treat."

I thank him, distractedly, for his gift, interested only in whom the letter is from. Relief overwhelms me when I see my mother's handwriting. I automatically open the envelope, while Victor strokes Boudine. Inside, I find a greetings card with a Post-it note stuck on it.

> *I wasn't sure whether to send this to you,*
> *but it arrived here for you. It's from Jérémy.*
> *Don't read it if you don't want to.*
> *Much love, Mom.*

On the card there's a golden stag in the snow and the message "Season's Greetings."

> *My angel,*
> *I'm counting every minute keeping us*
> *from our marriage. Can't wait for us to be*
> *united for life. I understand your doubts,*
> *they're normal before such a commitment.*
> *Call me, I'll know how to reassure you.*
> *Love you more than my own life.*
> *Jérémy*

55
JEANNE

When she got home, Jeanne found Iris picking at a *pain au chocolat*. Thankfully, she didn't ask her about her supposed appointment at the ophthalmologist's—Jeanne had never been able to lie. She preferred to keep quiet about her meetings with the medium, not wanting anyone to dissuade her from continuing with them. The séances put a strain on her finances, but she had got a decent price for several pieces of gold jewelry. Once at the jeweler's, she'd almost decided not to sell them. Some had sentimental value, like her baptism medal, and a bangle Pierre had given her, but she preferred to keep a link with her husband in the present, rather than keep objects from the past.

She exchanged a few words with Iris, who seemed no keener to chat than she was, and went to her room, hand deep in her jacket pocket, touching the envelope she had just received.

The letters had become less frequent recently. And were all the more precious for that. She settled into the armchair near her bed, made Boudine clamber up onto her knees, and began to read.

Winter 2015

Jeanne has just had her final session of chemotherapy. For months, she's been fighting breast cancer. Pierre has accompanied her to every session, every examination, every appointment. For the first time since her hair fell out, Jeanne has gone outdoors without a wig. Her hair has started to grow back, and she's decided not to dye it anymore. It's a pretty, silvery gray color. They return from hospital on foot, and walking feels so good to Jeanne, knowing that she's got several days of unpleasant side-effects to get through. On the way, they meet a neighbor, Madame Partelle. She knows that Jeanne is ill, but can't refrain from commenting on her haircut, which she finds masculine. Jeanne daren't respond, that's not her style. It's not Pierre's style, either, but he's cut to the quick by this attack on his wife, and responds sharply. "It takes a lot of class to wear a masculine haircut. For that reason, I'd advise you against trying it."

Jeanne smiles as she recalls what happened next. The neighbor had blanched, pursed her lips and continued on her way without a word. Pierre and Jeanne had chortled like kids who have just played a naughty trick on someone. The neighbor had never responded to their greetings again.

How she had always laughed with Pierre! They shared that sense of ridicule of those who'd never had the choice. He was her best audience, and she his. They would often compare themselves with others of their age, and realize that only their bodies had grown old. They saw themselves as children trapped in adult frames, and certainly had no desire to get out of them.

Jeanne was about to fold up the letter when something stopped her. She reread the letter slowly, pausing at each sentence to try to pin down what was bothering her. She stumbled over the eighth sentence, read it once more, before understanding. She knew who the sender was.

56
Théo

It's the big day. The competition is taking place at the Fermade school of bakery, in Courbevoie. I'd planned to take the metro, but Philippe insisted on driving me there. It's the first time I see him outside of the bakery, feels weird. Leïla wasn't working today, so she wanted to come along, too. I sat in the passenger seat, not daring to admit that the backseat made me nauseous. I couldn't eat a thing this morning anyhow, due to nerves, so I had to minimize the risk.

Philippe must think he can pile it on, because he casually tells me that if I get through this round and win the next one, I'll be automatically selected for the national competition.

"I didn't tell you before so as not to freak you out, but now you're bound to find out."

"You're right, now's a great time to tell me."

I feel Leïla's hand on my shoulder. It's there for just a few seconds, I don't get time to react. I glance into the rear-view mirror, Iris smiles at me, Jeanne watches the scenery go by. They, too, insisted on being there. I feel crazily stressed out, and know that's no good for me. I try to empty my mind, but that's even worse.

We're around thirty apprentices, and I feel like it's only my butt-cheeks that are quivering. Either they're all really calm, or they're better than me at stopping the façade from cracking when the inside is quaking. We wait a while in the courtyard, there's a delay because some judge hasn't arrived yet. I'm the only one who's come with four people, the rest are either alone, or just with the baker they're apprenticed to. It's a bit embarrassing, but for the one time it's this way around, I'm not going to complain.

The door opens, we can go in. The guy that takes my name

says only one person can accompany me, Philippe gives me no choice, he'll be by my side.

Leïla squeezes my shoulder again, and this time I lay my hand on hers. Iris wishes me good luck, Jeanne tells me to "go piss them right off."

There are name labels stuck on the large tables. All the equipment needed for the test is right there, while the ingredients, ovens, fridges, freezers, and electrical appliances for everyone's use are in a corner of the room. The judges on the panel introduce themselves, I don't know any of them, but I'm so anxious I'd forget my own name. The test is revealed: we have to make a lemon meringue tart. Philippe gives me a final word of encouragement and goes to sit at the back of the room with the other supporters.

"Three, two, one, off you go!"

I start with the sugar-crust pastry, I mix the ingredients, knead the dough and put it aside to chill. Meanwhile, I tackle the filling. I zest the lemon, cut it in half to squeeze it, nick my finger, see one drop of blood, then two, then a trickle, my ears start buzzing, it's hot in here, oh, stars, night-night little ones.

On the drive home, no one speaks. Philippe's teeth remain clenched. When I came round in the competition room, he insisted I carry on, but the organizers reckoned I looked too weak, and I didn't contradict them. I don't know if it was intentional, but the moment he switches on the car radio, Jean-Jacques Goldman is singing about cutting skin until it bleeds.

I don't look up from my phone for the entire journey. I'm dying of shame, but also relieved it's over. I'm watching a video when a message pops up. It's Leïla, who's sitting right behind me.

"Conquering your fear is already a big deal. You did what you could."

"Thanks. Philippe looks livid."

"That's his normal face lol. If you like, we could have a drink on Saturday night."

"That's kind, but I don't need pity."

"It's not pity, I want to."

57
Iris

"I asked you not to give him my number."

"But I felt sorry for him."

Conversations with my mother should be contraindicated during pregnancy. If my blood pressure doesn't soar now, there's a bad connection somewhere.

Since Jérémy's first message, she's denied giving him my number. She succeeded in making me have doubts, despite the evidence: only she, my brother, and Mel have it, and the last two wouldn't bat an eyelid at Jérémy's bleating. Finally, she's just admitted to talking regularly with him, and even having him in the house, twice.

"He doesn't understand why you left. And I must say, I don't, either. The wedding's soon now, darling, you can't leave all the guests in the lurch like that!"

"Mom, I deliberately didn't involve you, I don't want you worrying. Please, keep out of all this. And don't give him any more info! You didn't tell him I'm in Paris?"

Silence.

"Mom? Say you didn't tell him that."

"Oh, come on, the one time you landed on a nice boy! Your father liked him a lot, you know?"

I cut the call and hurl my phone across the room. I'm furious one minute, anxious the next. I knew she'd worry, but never thought it would be for him. My mother still sees me as a child who needs protection, incapable of sensible opinions and decisions. Hers trump mine. She knows better, she's the adult.

In the sitting room, on my way to the kitchen, I find Jeanne busy sewing.

"Everything okay?" she asks. "I wasn't spying, but I heard some shouting."

"Nothing serious, a row with my mother. She drives me crazy."

Jeanne smiles:

"Mine sometimes made me fly off the handle, I think it takes a mother to find our sensitive spots. In a few years' time, it's you who'll be driving your son crazy!"

"I think that's already the case—he moves so much, he must want to escape."

Jeanne laughs, but then her eyes cloud over:

"Does it hurt?"

"No, it just feels weird. But when he kicks my ribs, that is uncomfortable. Do you want to see?"

The suggestion pulls her up short, I instantly regret it.

"Sorry, I didn't mean to . . ."

"I'd love to!" she cuts in, standing up.

I stretch out on the sofa, the position in which my baby shows himself the most. I lift up my sweatshirt, revealing the taut skin over my belly. For a few minutes, we wait for a sign of life.

"It's always like that," I say. "At night, when I want to sleep, he takes my uterus for a trampoline, but whenever I want to video him, he hides."

"He's going to be a rascal," murmurs Jeanne. "May I?"

With a nod, I encourage her to place her hand near my navel. I sense that she's moved. I am, too.

"It's the first time," she admits.

And that's the moment my dear child chooses to do a somersault, creating a moving bulge under Jeanne's hand. Her eyes widen and she cries out:

"That's incredible! Extraordinary! To think there's a little being under there. Life is amazing."

The door opens on Théo, who'd been out since early afternoon. He observes us from a distance, intrigued by this bizarre spectacle.

"What are you doing?"

"Come and see," Jeanne whispers to him. "It's magical."

He obeys, approaches us, eyes riveted on my belly. A surge of movement pushes out my skin, Théo steps back:

"Shit, that's gross! It's like some alien."

58
JEANNE

On her way back from the cemetery, Jeanne stopped off at Théo's bakery to buy a Black Forest gâteau. It was her seventy-fifth birthday and she intended to tell no one, but every year on that day, she liked to relive how she felt as a child. Her mother, knowing Jeanne's love of chocolate, would always make her the same Black Forest gâteau, even if, as Jeanne grew bigger, the cake seemed increasingly small. She was queen for the day and, exceptionally, had the privilege of being served first, instead of her father. Since Louise wasn't keen on the chocolate shavings around the cake, and Jeanne was happy to give up her cherries, the two sisters would do a swap, closely watched by their dog Caprice, who was hoping for a few crumbs on the way. Decades later, with just a mouthful of sponge cake and Chantilly cream, Jeanne was eight years old again.

True to form, the woman at the bakery kept any cordiality to herself, and Jeanne admired Théo for putting up with such a colleague.

As Jeanne returned home, she was planning supper in her head. At the bottom of the stairs, she hesitated for a few seconds and then made for Victor's apartment. She took a few more moments to think, then knocked on the door.

Boudine dived into the hall as soon as he opened it. At Victor's invitation, Jeanne followed her in. It wasn't unusual for her to stop by and have a coffee with him, so he didn't seem surprised by this impromptu visit.

"It's too late for coffee," the caretaker declared, opening the fridge, "but I should have some lemonade, or some rosé."

"I'm not staying," Jeanne told him, "I have a cake to put in the fridge. I've just come to pick your memory. Do you remember Madame Partelle?"

Victor answered immediately:

"Of course! Madame Partelle, on the first floor. She moved to Brittany, if I'm not mistaken. There've been so many residents, it's hard not to get them mixed up. Why do you ask?"

Jeanne opened her bag, took out the little collection of letters she'd received, and placed it on the table:

"Because she was called Madame Pardelle, not Partelle. You always got her name wrong."

Victor's hand went up to his face and he rubbed his forehead. Jeanne could see the conflict in his eyes: should he confess, or pretend not to understand?

He was born in 1972, three years after Jeanne and Pierre moved into their apartment. His mother, Madame Giuliano, had taken over as caretaker from her parents. His father, who worked at the local butcher's, had died young. The child had grown up in the building, never far from his adored mother. It had become a bit of a joke, with the residents always asking Madame Giuliano, when little Victor wasn't with her, if he was hidden under her skirt. He was a polite, helpful and witty child, qualities that had endeared him to everyone. Pierre and Jeanne had become particularly fond of him, even welcoming him into their home. Pierre had given him English lessons during his middle-school years, and Jeanne had introduced him to sewing. He had turned into an absent-minded adolescent, often with his head in the clouds, and then an isolated young man, who hadn't integrated into any stratum of society. He only felt safe and happy in his little apartment on the ground floor. When his mother had died, four years ago, Victor had naturally taken up the baton.

"I thought it might do you some good," he muttered, "I saw in a TV program that reliving happy memories helped with grieving."

"How did you know about all these anecdotes?"

"You know how good my memory is, and sharp my ears! I hear everything, I remember everything. For example, that story about Madame Partelle—or Pardelle—you told to my mother when you got back. I was there, I can still hear your laughter."

Jeanne had forgotten that detail

"I'm really sorry if I upset you," Victor whispered.

"You didn't upset me, don't you worry. I know that you loved him a lot, too."

He nodded his head, silently. Jeanne meant what she said. Not only was she not angry with Victor, but she was also deeply moved. He must be pretty attached to her, and touched by her grief, to go to such lengths to ease it. The attachment was mutual. Victor mattered to Jeanne. He had given her a lovely proof of friendship, but above all, the most wonderful of presents: memories with Pierre.

Jeanne left shortly afterwards, once Boudine had found all of the cat's scattered snacks. The caretaker went with her to the door.

"Victor, please . . . "

"Yes?"

"Would you mind sending me some more letters?"

He agreed to, and Jeanne left his apartment with a smile on her lips.

THÉO

"When you coming over, bro?"

Since I've started replying to messages from Gérard and Ahmed, they've been badgering me to visit them. Gégé will be eighteen in a month's time, and Ahmed still has six months to wait. When I was in their position, I wanted just one thing: to get the hell out of that kids' home, which to me was a prison. At eighteen, you have no choice, whether you've got somewhere to go or not, you have to leave. I know some who became homeless afterwards. Many. That's why I didn't want to go to uni, or whatever, I had to earn some dough. As an apprentice, it's no fortune, but it's something.

I don't know why I don't feel like going back there. Maybe because of the bad memories, maybe because of the other memories. With some distance, the good times do feature a little more in my memory. On the day I left, Ahmed picked up a guitar and they all sang a farewell song to me. Several of them had got together to write the words, recalling things I'd been through there. I clenched my fists really tight and managed to keep my blubbering inside me. Gérard gave me the cap he always wore, some little ones hugged me, Manon cried.

There were some really tough times. For years, Sébastien, a youth worker, treated us like dogs, or worse. He made sure he hit us in places where it didn't show. I was small, I didn't dare defend myself, but even the big guys didn't take him on. Some other kids placed in the home were violent, I got hit around the face quite a bit for no reason, had things I cared about swiped from me, there were screams, escapes, and even suicide attempts. But I think the most painful was the hoping. The hope that my mother would visit me, the hope she'd quit drinking, the hope she'd take me back. One day, a shrink told me that I was better off at the kids' home than at my mother's. I insulted him and left. I couldn't hear that. I loved my mother like all kids do: unconditionally. I just wanted to be with her. I'll never know if he was right, if it was better to be alone but protected, or with her but in danger.

There were the good times. Nico and Assa, two youth workers who treated me like their little brother. The ball games while putting the world to rights. The evenings when we'd sneak out, well, those when we didn't get caught. Giggling in the showers, when we'd sing at the top of our voices. The TV evenings. That time we went to the beach. The skating rink. Ahmed and Gérard, my brothers. Manon. Malik, Sonia, Enzo, Emma. When you share the same hardship, it creates bonds, whether you like it or not. Even when there's no one to receive it, we have love to give. It wasn't really a family but, sometimes, it was a good imitation of one.

I reply to the message with some bullshit and turn off my phone. It's past midnight. I switch off the light, slide under the comforter and close my eyes. In my head, there's a place I take refuge in as soon as I feel the need. Like a parallel world, an imaginary life, where I risk nothing, where all ends well. An anteroom to real life, in which it's me who decides. I thought everyone had a place like that, but whenever I mentioned it to those around me, I realized there weren't that many of us. I stopped talking about it. It started when I was really little. I can still see myself, lying on my bed, enjoying an end-of-year show in which I dare to sing in front of everyone. I can just close my eyes and I find myself elsewhere, far from all the hassle, far from what's in store. It's escapism without a book or a screen. A personal one-reeler. For a while now, the same film has been showing. I arrive early at the bakery. I have the keys, I go inside and change in the cloakroom. I'm stripped to the waist, I have the body of a firefighter pin-up. Leïla walks into the room, slowly comes up to me, slides her hand around the nape of my neck, and kisses me.

"I missed you so much."

"You're suffocating me."

I relax my grip and take a look at my brother, there in flesh and blood before me.

"Ow! You're wacko, why d'you pinch me?"

"To be sure I'm not dreaming."

I took the bus to go and meet him at the airport. I hadn't told him. He walked right past without recognizing me. If I weren't as happy to see him again, I'd have taken it badly.

For the entire return journey, he tells me about his travels, the people he met, all backed up with photos and videos. I've seen most on his Instagram account, but his stories could captivate a tree.

The hotel he has booked into is just a few minutes from the apartment. He drops his bag on the floor and turns towards me, staring at my bump:

"I can't get over it. I'm going to be an uncle."

"I'm getting scared, you know. In less than three months, he'll be here."

"What are you scared of?"

"Everything. Of losing him, of him being ill, of Jérémy asking for custody, of my son reproaching me for depriving him of a father, of not being up to the task. The closer it gets, the more I think I won't make it."

Expressing these fears makes them real. For weeks, I've refused to open the door to them and let them overwhelm me. I'm always quick to question everything, doubt weighs me down. I blame myself for anything negative that happens to me, and thank my lucky stars for anything positive. Little by little, as much due to failures as successes, my confidence increased. And also due to being surrounded by people who believed in me when I didn't. Jérémy was one of those, at first.

He understood me, listened to me, was interested in how I felt. He would encourage me, often excessively. Anything I did was an excuse to shower me in praise. A risotto? The best he'd eaten in all his life. A new hairstyle? Everything suited me, I'd look great with a shaved head. A new patient? I would fix them, I was the most gifted physio. Between his too much and my not enough, there was a happy medium that kept me stable. The downward slide was insidious. I remember the first comment that stunned me.

"It's overcooked. You should take some lessons from my ex."

I cried, he apologized: he was stressed over a contract that had just slipped through his fingers. He returned to being the man I loved. And then another slap in the face.

"When we make love, all I can see is your double chin."

And another; another; another. "Those jeans give you a fat ass"; "You're so not funny"; "Once people realize, no one will pick you as their physio anymore"; "God you can be dumb"; "I rue the day I asked you to come and live here"; "Never wonder why your friends don't speak to you anymore?" "You really are useless."

The criticism shrouded the compliments. The problem being that I would believe the former more than the latter.

Each attack was followed by consolation. It wasn't meant badly, it was for my own good, he was so sorry it hurt me, that wasn't the intention. By repairing what he'd broken, he became indispensable. He was my torturer and my savior. The knife and the bandage. It didn't take long for me to believe more in him than in myself. To convince myself that, without him, I was capable of nothing. That he alone could understand me. Love me. Over three years, he succeeded in demolishing what I'd spent thirty years building.

"You're going to be a brilliant mother," my brother assures me. "And I should know, you treated me like your own child for years."

I laugh, thinking back to the time when I would copy my mother, to the extent of even trying to breastfeed baby Clément.

"I'll do all I can."

My brother sits down beside me on the bed and rests his head on my shoulder.

"I'm in love," he says, suddenly.

Even my baby is surprised by the news.

"You? No way! Who with? Where? When? Tell me everything, I've been waiting for this for twenty-eight years!"

Clément has never introduced anyone to me, or mentioned a possible love affair. When I used to question him on the subject, he would just shrug his shoulders with a smile. It drove me crazy, when I couldn't resist sharing the merest flicker of a romance with him. On several occasions, I overheard calls, noticed changes, spotted small things, but I respected his discretion, convinced that he'd choose his moment. I really thought it would never arrive. She's called Camille, is a photographer in Buenos Aires, and has accompanied Clément on his travels for more than year. They plan to move in together, either here or elsewhere. It's subtle, almost imperceptible, but when he talks about her, something lights up in his eyes, his voice softens, his gestures become expansive. I admire, as a spectator, my loved-up brother. It was worth waiting for.

61
JEANNE

Little Jeanne had been brought up to respect others. The rules were simple: others ruled. You mustn't bother others, disappoint others, disturb others, annoy others, tire others, delay others, hurry others, hurt others, upset others, hinder others. To meet expectations, Jeanne had soon adopted certain behaviors, donned them like clothes, and stifled her natural character.

Big Jeanne had, over the years and with maturity, managed to remove several layers of artifice, but some were so deeply engrained they had become part of her skin. Thus, when Jeanne was annoyed, she would lock away her feelings and put on a perfectly convincing smile for anyone she encountered. You had to know her well to detect the annoyance behind the mask. Théo and Iris were, indeed, starting to know her well.

"Jeanne, are you angry with us?" Iris asked, anxiously, sitting beside her on the sofa.

"Absolutely not," Jeanne replied.

"It's obvious something's bothering you," Théo insisted.

"I'm telling you, I'm totally fine."

They looked at each other, both hoping that they had done the right thing.

It had all started with that call. The landline phone had rung in the middle of supper. This rarely happened, and it was always Jeanne who answered. She was busy in the kitchen, so Iris had picked up. A man had asked to speak to Madame Perrin, Jeanne had taken the receiver, and the other two had soon got the gist of the conversation. Returning to the table, Jeanne had felt obliged to reveal her secret.

"I'm seeing a medium."

"To look into the future?" Théo had asked.

Jeanne had remained vague, before admitting that she was communicating with her dear husband with the aid of a professional. Iris had been all for it—her friend Gaëlle had talked with her late father in the same way. Although dubious at first, Gaëlle had been convinced by the details provided by the medium, details which only she knew.

"Some people really do have a gift," Iris had concluded, "but you have to be careful, there are lots of charlatans, too. The authentic ones are easily identified: they have a long waiting list and people come from far away to see them."

"I was very lucky," Jeanne had responded. "He contacted me directly, I didn't have to wait."

Théo had grimaced:

"How did he contact you?"

"By phone. It's Pierre who dictated our number to him."

"Shit," Iris had said. "That reminds me of Madame Beaulieu, my patient who died two months ago. When I went to pick up my gown and a meal box a few days later, her daughter told me that a medium had called her at home to say that her mother had a message for her. She'd slammed the phone down on him. Really weird."

"Yup," Théo had agreed. "That stinks."

Jeanne had let nothing show, but she regretted having confided in them. Many inconsistencies and contradictions had already dented her confidence in this Monsieur Kafka, she wouldn't allow more doubt to be instilled into her mind.

"I'm so sorry if I upset you," Iris added, getting up from the sofa. "He might be really good. Probably is, even. You're best placed to know, we've never seen him."

Jeanne relaxed, but Théo wasn't done:

"We could do."

"Do what?" asked Jeanne.

"See him! Then we could tell you what we think. When's your next appointment?"

62
THÉO

It's not yet ten o'clock. I hide in the street behind the bar so she won't know I was early. Since Leïla suggested we have a drink, I've almost passed out every time I've been near her, without even cutting my finger. I've barely slept a wink at night, and even in my imaginary world, I've been stressed out.

It's my first ever date. With Manon, the kiss just happened, well, particularly for her, I went along with it as if it were perfectly normal, while inside I was whooping it up. We were as crazy as each other, listened to the same music, and her eyes were awesome: at fifteen, that's like winning the lottery. Before her, I'd had a quick fling with a girl in my class, bussing in the bike shed so no one would see us. She said that was out of respect, I think it was out of shame. And that's it. Must say, I've never been inundated with offers. This is the first time I'm going on a first date.

And even better, it's the first time I've got a date with a girl I already like a lot.

I smoke a final cig while counting my heartbeats, and they're far too fast for a human heart.

"Hi!"

I jump, Leïla is right in front of me. My heart doesn't even pause between beats now. I'm running on direct current.

"Hi!" I say back. "You okay?"

It's a great start, I'm as riveting as a bank statement.

The bar is quiet. We sit at the back of the room, at a high table. Leïla seems as intimidated as me. We have a first drink, talk about this and that, I learn that she's lived alone for six months, having previously lived with her parents and brother and sister. She's soon to be twenty. She combines three jobs: the bakery, office cleaning, and shifts at her brother's restaurant.

"And you? The lady who came to the competition, is she your grandmother?"

"No, I share an apartment with her and Iris."

Her eyebrows go up. Here we go. I must now decide whether to tell the truth, or invent some other person. Coming from a kids' home has always set me apart. People behave differently once they find out. At school, I was the guy who had no parents. Either no one came near me, or if they did, it was out of curiosity or pity. I sometimes felt like an animal in a zoo. I was exotic. Leïla is waiting for me to explain. I turn the words over in my head, trying to put them in order. I know they could change everything.

"I come from Brive. I don't earn enough to pay for my own apartment, and I didn't know anyone in Paris. I don't have a family, I grew up in a kids' home."

I daren't look at her. I stare at my glass, holding my breath.

"They both seem cool," she finally says. "They were really concerned about you, I thought they were family. Shall we make a move?"

She didn't react. Didn't ask any questions. Didn't want to know why, how. Either it's a non-subject for her, or she didn't hear, or she couldn't care less.

We're back on the pavement, it's cold, our breath is foggy. I'm just plucking up courage to ask her if she actually heard me, when she indicates for me to follow her:

"Come, I'm going to show you something."

We walk along the Seine, exchanging stories about Nathalie, an inexhaustible subject, and we can't stop laughing.

"'No, sir, we don't give credit,'" Leïla mimics. "'You can see I'm not wearing a sari, so don't confuse me with Mother Teresa!'"

"You do her *so* well!"

"I know, I know, I'm gifted like that."

She stops in front of the door of a building and taps in the code, explaining that she cleans an office on the top floor. We find ourselves in a private courtyard, she puts her finger to her lips for me to keep quiet. I follow her up the stairs, right to the top. There's a wooden ladder leaning against the wall, she takes it and places it under a trapdoor in the ceiling. She whispers to me to climb up after her.

The view takes my breath away. Literally. My legs are shaking and my head's spinning. We can see all of Paris, its roofs stretching out to infinity. In the distance, the Eiffel Tower, and closer up, the Sacré Coeur. Leïla walks a few steps along the ridge of the roof, I cling to a large pipe and slide down to the floor.

"Shit, are you okay?" she asks, coming to sit beside me.

"Yes, yes, I'm great. Got a defibrillator on you?"

She bursts out laughing, and when she's done, we listen to the night for a long while. Gradually, I stop shaking and almost forget that I'm on top of a building. Leïla doesn't move, I'd like to know what she's thinking. I take a deep breath and go for it:

"Did you hear what I told you in the bar?"

"Yes, I heard. I know it's a difficult subject for you. I know because I have my own difficult subjects. We've plenty of time to talk about them, when we feel like it."

The shaking starts up again, I've still got vertigo, but it's a different kind this time. Leïla looks at me, her face is a breath away, I put my fears aside, close my eyes, and we kiss.

(I'm surprised the Eiffel Tower doesn't put on a firework display for the occasion.)

63
Iris

Jeanne didn't agree to it. We didn't insist, it was up to her whether she preferred to delude herself or accept reality. But yesterday, at supper, she admitted to us that she'd changed her mind. She wanted to know for sure.

When he opens the door, the medium looks surprised that Jeanne isn't alone. I hold my hand out to him:

"Hello, I'm Madame Perrin's daughter."

"And I'm her grandson, her daughter's son," adds Théo, nodding in my direction.

I nearly choke. The little twit is pleased with himself.

This is the first test. Jeanne told us that Monsieur Kafka knew that she'd not had children. But he doesn't react. I give him the benefit of the doubt.

The medium invites us to sit at a round table. The room itself is a pastiche. All that's missing is the crystal ball and the potion made from the ovaries of dwarf hamsters. I remember Gaëlle's description of her first appointment with her medium. She'd been surprised at how sober the place was, far from the theatrical setting she'd expected. I glance at Jeanne. With head held high and a frank expression, she lets none of her torment show.

"You said you'd received a new message from Pierre?"

"Absolutely!" says Monsieur Kafka, livening up. "It's rare for the deceased to contact me so often, he seems very attached to you."

Jeanne smiles. My desire to unmask the man has gone, I want him to be sincere. Want him not to say these words, which would move anyone desperately missing someone, just for money. I daren't imagine how she must feel, torn between hope and reason.

"I'm going to repeat directly what he says to me," the medium continues. "Don't worry, I keep my own voice, but it's definitely him speaking through me. So, here we go."

He throws his head back and places his index fingers on his temples:

"Hello my darling, you're looking very beautiful today. I'm so happy to have found this way to communicate with you. Thank you for believing in Monsieur Kafka. We're lucky we can maintain this link. I'm with you all the time. At night, I lie beside you in our apartment in the Rue des Batignolles, like before. I love you, my darling. I hope to be able to speak to you even more often."

Jeanne's cheeks are streaming with tears. She pulls a hankie from her sleeve, dabs her eyes, and slowly turns towards us:

"You were right, children."

Théo needs no more encouragement.

"Is he here?" he asks Monsieur Kafka.

"Absolutely. Your grandfather is right beside you. Maybe you can feel his hand on your shoulder."

Théo closes his eyes and breathes in deeply.

"I can feel it," he whispers, reopening them. "I was very close to him. I called him Fatso."

The medium stares at an imaginary point in space:

"He remembers that clearly. He loved you calling him that. He had a particular soft spot for you. Don't tell the others!"

Jeanne is impassive. I move my chair closer to her and put my hand over hers.

"Does he have a message for me?"

The man resumes his stance. After a few seconds, with his eyes fixed on my belly, he replies:

"Your daddy asks me to tell you that he's happy that life's going on for you. He regrets not having had time to meet the latest little one, but promises to watch over him from above."

He's very good. Jeanne's distress breaks my heart.

"Well, I'm pleased he died before," says Théo, "or I'd have had to share my inheritance. Since he can hear me, I thank him for leaving me his fortune. There's so much money, I don't know what to do with it all. Maybe he'd have some advice for me?"

"Of course!" the medium is quick to reply. "Your Fatso would be delighted to help you through me. We'll make an appointment at the end of the séance, if you like?"

"O.K.! Ask him now what he thinks of my first investment."

Théo is scaring me, I don't know where he's going with this. Monsieur Kafka listens in silence, nodding his head:

"He's proud of you. He congratulates you on such a responsible investment."

"Ah, I'm relieved! I thought he'd find it trivial. But it was worth it, I gained ten centimeters when flaccid, it's powerful stuff. When I'm standing, I feel like a tripod. It's really useful: if I break a leg, no big deal, I can walk with my dick!"

The man smiles, excessively. I bite the inside of my cheeks so as not to laugh. Jeanne suddenly sits up:

"Oh my God, what's happening to me?"

"Jeanne, what is it?"

"I don't know, it's strange, I can see a woman standing behind Monsieur Kafka. I think I'm seeing a vision!"

Théo's look of bewilderment right then is unforgettable.

"A vision?" the medium asks, incredulous.

"Yes, you must have passed your gift on to me!" she cries. "It's your mother, she has a message for you. She'd like to know if you're not ashamed of taking advantage of people's distress to line your pockets."

"What are you talking about?"

"Wait, my vision isn't over! I see you plunging your hand into your drawer and reimbursing me the one thousand euros I gave you."

The man's smile collapses. He's offended, doesn't understand why he should return money that was honestly earnt. Jeanne is impressively calm.

"I've understood how you found me. You go through the obituary column, pick the elderly widows, then find out their contact details."

"That's awful," Théo adds. "You deserve to be KO'd by me, using my third leg."

Jeanne stares coldly at Kafka:

"If you don't want me to lodge a complaint, you'll have to reimburse me, bro."

It's not enough to convince him. This isn't his first attempt, and others before us must have unmasked him. He pleads sincerity, and we have no way of proving his dishonesty.

On the journey home, Théo keeps clowning around, and I keep trying to start a conversation. Jeanne responds to neither of us. Back at the apartment, she asks us to sit on either side of her on the sofa, switches on the TV, covers our legs with a rug, rests her head on the back of the sofa, then grips my hand and Théo's tightly in hers.

64
JEANNE

As Jeanne entered the atelier, the memories flooded back. Some faces had changed, but the smells, sounds, and look of the place were the same as ever. Those who knew her immediately left their seats to come and greet her. Viviane, the head seamstress for floaty styles, gave her a long hug. Jeanne remembered her arrival, in 1980, or maybe '81, the year of the presidential elections. Viviane was a young thing then, and now she was close to retiring. Luis, Marianne, Clotilde, Paul and the others formed a circle around her, and Jeanne was amazed to feel as if she'd left them only yesterday.

Despite her promises, she hadn't stayed in contact with any of her former colleagues. During the first few weeks after she'd left, she'd dropped in to say hello a few times, but the fear of disturbing them held her back. They were working, after all, and her visit would just distract them. She had gone from every day to never. A few phone calls had continued, before, in turn, fading away as daily life and new plans took over.

Jeanne was quick to explain the purpose of her visit. She needed the management's permission, which didn't prove difficult, and her proposal was met with enthusiasm by everyone. She had thought of it the previous night, while waiting for sleep to come. She had stopped relying on sleeping pills for the past three weeks, and although her nights were calmer, she wasn't quite there yet. Between darker thoughts, Jeanne had found herself thinking back to all the offcuts of fabric thrown away at the atelier every day. It was no big deal to them, nothing could be done with such scraps. But for others, nothing was a lot. First thing in the morning, she had knocked on the door of one of the charities she sometimes supported.

Jeanne got down to work as soon as she was back home, and only left her sewing machine to go to visit Pierre. She returned to it in the evening, and the following day, and the day after that. The caress of the fabric and the purr of the machine, along with the hope of being useful, filled her with joy. A feeling she had feared never finding again. Jeanne had always had a pronounced taste for happiness. It was her nature, she didn't glory in it, quite the reverse, she felt lucky to have the gift of being so easily delighted, which balanced out her darker side. She had often reflected on how the two sides were linked, the certainty of one's transience just magnifying the small joys. Although the ordeals she had faced along the way might have dented her optimism, they hadn't made it disappear altogether. When Pierre had died, a light had gone out, and, she felt sure, would never come on again. After lengthy hibernation, Jeanne could feel herself coming back to life.

She folded the garment she had just finished sewing and placed it in the large basket with the rest. Tomorrow, she would donate it all to the charity, before making some more. Soon, some chubby little hands would be clutching at bibs, toys, security blankets, sleepsuits, coverlets made of taffeta, jacquard, brocade or organza.

65
Théo

I didn't tell anyone I was coming. I wasn't sure I'd be able to go through with it. I walk around the perimeter, along the wire fence, and recognize the holes we'd squeeze through when escaping. There's still one left that hasn't been closed up. I hear them before I see them. The little ones are playing in groups in the yard. The older ones are chatting and kicking around a ball. Ahmed is sitting on the ping-pong table. I whistle, he instantly swivels around, and then charges over to me, whooping.

Nico lets me in, it feels strange going through this door. Everyone gathers around me, I'm given slaps on the back, kisses, and a big cuddle from Mayline, a little one who liked being around me. Apparently, I resemble her father. There are some new arrivals, who hang back a little. I'm not really sure how I feel, it's all mixed up, but I can't stop smiling. It's like some TV cross-over, when two series combine for just one episode. I feel as if my old life is making an appearance in my new life, and the episode has started well.

Ahmed tells me that Gérard is in the bedroom, so we charge in without knocking and pile on top of him. He's listening to music through his earbuds, doesn't know what's happening, fights back, and when he sees me, cracks up laughing. Ahmed does, too, still sounding like a billy goat, and then it's my turn. On the wall above his bed, he's stuck a photo of us three at the skating rink. We were thirteen or fourteen, spent more time on our asses than on the skates, and I left a little of my pride there, but it remains one of my best memories.

Ahmed was three when he arrived at the home, along with his big sister. Their mother had just died and their father didn't have the means to bring them up properly. Gérard arrived two years after me. He had been taken from his parents because they abused him. He never gave any details, but still bore the marks on his body and in his head. Sometimes there's a waiting-room for friendship, but with those two, it was straight in.

We stay together for two or three hours, just hanging out like before. They ask me loads of questions on life after the home, we'd seen so many turn out badly, they want to believe in it, so I put the best spin on things. When you have nightmares in your rear-view mirror, you move forward aiming for dreams. I tell them about work, the apartment, Jeanne, Iris, and I don't need to tell them about Leïla, they figure it out themselves when we come across Manon. She and I give each other a peck on the cheek, exchange a few words, and search as I might, I feel nothing inside. No fluttering, no knot in my stomach, no lump in my throat. I'm pleased to see her, and it stops there. My convalescence from her is over.

They make me promise to come back soon, and even if they hadn't, I would have. I don't know how I thought I could leave them in the past.

Visiting time will soon be over, but I can't be this close to my mother without stopping by to see her. I tell her about my relationship with Jeanne and Iris, which has taken an unexpected turn. By sharing the apartment, I thought I'd find tranquility, but I've found much more than that. I tell her she would have liked them, just as she would have liked Leïla. My mother always preferred people with flaws to those without. She'd often say that two smooth surfaces slide over each other, whereas two dented surfaces catch onto each other and become stronger together. She wasn't always wrong.

Before going, I stick another photo up on her wall. In the corridor, I walk behind a family who are leaving. A lady with her two sons, no doubt there to visit a loved one. Without thinking, I turn back, open the door to my mother's room, lean close to her ear, and admit to her what I've done, and what I'm about to do.

66
Iris

It's my last day of work before maternity leave. Nadia welcomes me with a tray covered in little cakes.

"Do you think I'm expecting octuplets, or what?" I ask her.

"Try one, you'll thank me for making so many."

I'm relieved to be stopping work. My belly is so heavy, I'm wondering if my son will be born driving a tank. I anticipate a hectic schedule for the days to come, what with napping, reading, and more napping. However, Jeanne seemed so pleased to hear that that I'd soon be in the apartment all day that I'm expecting to have to add a few games of Yahtzee and Scrabble to my timetable.

I kept on with the viewings after moving in with her. I didn't want to impose life with a baby on her, and all that that entails. I handed in my applications, whether the apartment suited me or not. Last week, I was chosen by the owner of a studio apartment, in Bagneux, from around twenty applicants. When I announced the news at supper, Jeanne turned into an inspector:

"The surface area?"

"Thirty-two square meters."

"Too small. The rent?"

"Seven hundred and twenty euros."

"Too expensive. Double glazing?"

"Single."

"Poor isolation from high and low temperatures, and noise. Which floor?"

None of my answers received her approval, and she ended up suggesting that I stay at hers until I found accommodation worthy of the name. I didn't try to hide my joy, I couldn't have. When I stood up to kiss her, Théo warned us that he'd leave the table if we started crying.

"I've met the person replacing you," Nadia tells me, while maneuvering her wheelchair in the hall. "She came with the boss of the agency. Well, it's going to be much more dullsville than with you. My son tried a little joke, and we almost had to resuscitate her."

"What kind of joke?"

"Nothing that bad. He left a plastic snake lying in the bath."

She laughs, remembering the scene, and I can't help but laugh with her, partly out of relief at not having been the target of this joke, no doubt. Just show me a snake, and my cervix will dilate.

Nadia doesn't leave me all afternoon. She follows me into every room and keeps asking me to sit down and stop cleaning. I finally do as she says, in front of a decaf.

"You won't be returning after your leave, will you?" she asks.

I shake my head:

"I'm going to try to go back to my real job."

Nadia sighs, with a smile. I've been coming here five days a week for over six months. I've entered a private world. I've been close to vulnerability. I've seen the flaws, the fears, the strength, the rawness. That creates bonds. I know that Monsieur Hamadi and Madame Lavoir, who replaced Madame Beaulieu, will often be in my thoughts. But Nadia is a special case. I'll miss her, the way only those who matter are missed. So, as she accompanies me to the front door, having first made me take the cakes I hadn't eaten with me, and asks if we could see each other again, I don't hesitate, and our farewells turn into promises.

February

67
JEANNE

As she bought a bunch of mimosa at the florist's, Jeanne found herself torn between two feelings. Life with her great love felt like it was just yesterday, and also felt like it was an eternity ago. All at once, she was both an open wound and healed over. Her emotions threw her onto a roller coaster, and she clung on with all her might to resist their paradoxical pull.

Yesterday, an eternity ago, Pierre had given her an armful of mimosa, the first flowers of the season. He remembered every year, knowing how Jeanne loved the little yellow pompons as much as their scent. She had some tricks to make them last as long as possible: she would crush the stem ends with a hammer, plunge them into slightly sweetened water in a transparent vase, moisten them several times a day with a mister, and put them in the kitchen, the apartment's lightest room. But most importantly, she would talk to them, gently and solemnly, which Pierre found hilarious.

Almost a year had gone by since that fatal day. Soon, the round of "first time since" events would be over.

On the bus, clutching her yellow bouquet, Jeanne had a fleeting thought: she had survived. Guilt immediately chased it away, but it had left its mark.

She never would have thought she'd outlive Pierre. How often had she told him so, without thinking that it could really happen to them? "I'll go before you, I couldn't do anything else." She had done something else. She had gone under, languished at the bottom, become familiar with the shadows. She had wanted to stay down there, alone, devasted, to die since living had lost its point. She had been told that time was her ally, that as it passed over her wounds, it would soothe them. She had refused to hear it. Grief was the last thing that linked her to him. And yet. Just as, each day, the sun stole a few seconds from the night, each day, life stole a few seconds from death.

She breathed in the scent of the mimosa, thinking, so it's true. One could survive anything.

That morning, Jeanne had stood in the pool of light in the middle of her room. Naked, arms outstretched like the meerkats Pierre was so fond of. Then she had done some sewing, to the sound of Brel, Barbara, and Céline Dion, one of the few contemporary singers to move her. Iris had got up late, as she often did since being on maternity leave. Jeanne had introduced her to *Desperate Housewives*, and they had watched two episodes in a row, commenting on Gabrielle's outfits and Bree's behavior with relish. \

Everyday life had returned to something resembling normal.

She would never be the same as she was before. She had been broken, and then repaired. Missing him wouldn't stop, she knew that, she didn't want it to. She was fragile, unsteady, but she was standing.

Simone wasn't there when she arrived at the cemetery, and neither was the man she'd befriended. Jeanne found herself smiling, and went off to replace the wilting tulips with the mimosa.

THÉO

Leïla asked me to come to her place to give her some bakery lessons. I was too bowled over by this to keep it to myself, so I told Jeanne and Iris about it, and soon regretted doing so. They wanted me to wear a shirt and old-fogy shoes, like I was going to a costume ball. They followed me onto the landing to cheer me on, and when I came out onto the pavement, they kept it up from the window. I feel as if I'm about to climb Everest. I acted like I was embarrassed, but in fact I was pleased.

We've only seen each other twice outside of work since our first kiss on the roof. The more I get to know her, the keener I am on her. I don't know if there's a limit, a ceiling, a peak, a day when things start to stagnate before sliding down again, but right now, I'm racing up towards love, and fucking loving it. At the bakery, we make sure no one picks up on it, but whenever we get the chance, we brush against each other, smile at each other, and other such little things. On days when she's not there, or when I'm at the training center, she's all I can think of. I've never felt this way, and, even if it does sometimes scare me, I'd like to stay in this state all my life. Everything's lighter, everything's less serious. I just wish my heart would quit turning into a pneumatic drill the minute I think of her, because it's going to end up bursting through my chest and out into the open.

I didn't put a shirt on, but I've brought flowers. Jeanne left me no choice—much as I told her that stuff like that was *so* last century, I sensed I couldn't go too far.

Leïla doesn't have a vase, so she fills her washbasin with water and sticks the bouquet in it. Her apartment is tiny, and the kitchen doesn't merit the name. I ask her where she'd like us to do the baking, and she blushes:

"I wasn't really thinking of baking."

"Oh? So what do you want to do?"

"Play Monopoly?" she suggests, laughing.

"Great idea!"

Seeing her look crestfallen, I twig. I think back to Jeanne and Iris, it seems I'm the last to have understood what I was coming here for.

My heart's killing me, I'm hot, I take off my sweater, Leïla puts herself in front of me and asks if I could take hers off.

I start with the sleeves, and when it comes to dumb ideas, this wins the prize. Leïla ends up with the sweater-neck stuck around her ears, and her outstretched arms trapped, while I tug like a donkey. The sweater finally comes off, and I think her ears may have come too, but she puts a brave face on it, if that's the right expression when her hair's now sticking up and her lipstick's shifted to her forehead. She presses herself to me, kisses me, every hair on my body stands on end, she pulls me to the sofa-bed.

"Wait a second, I'll unfold it."

I help her, we fall onto the sheets, joined at the lip, she takes off my T-shirt, then her own, I stroke her skin, it's soft, and never mind the spring digging into my ribs. She straddles me, I push down the straps of her bra, she tries to unfasten it, and, swept up in the romance of it all, I decide to give her a hand. What a joke. The same guy who invented easy-access packaging also came up with bra fasteners. You need a master's to work it out. Leïla laughs and does it herself. It's no longer a defibrillator I need, it's a miracle. I tell her she's stunning, she tells me she loves me, I tell her same here, and once I've passed the skinny jeans-removal test, we make love without passing Go.

69
IRIS

"Shall we go for a walk?"

Boudine reacts before Jeanne does. She charges off to the hall to wag her tail under the leash hanging from the wall. Jeanne turns off her sewing machine and puts her coat on. The gynecologist advised me to walk as much as possible to improve my circulation and avoid the water retention that's turned my legs into sausages. Every morning, I spend ten minutes pulling on support stockings, and ten more unstiffening my back post-maneuver.

The first time I suggested to Jeanne that she join me on my walk, I slowed my pace so as not to tire her out. Before we'd even reached the end of the street, she'd left me behind.

"I'm a Parisian," she declared, by way of explanation.

Since then, she has kept to my pace, which she says is slow, but I prefer to call leisurely.

Victor sticks his head out of the window to greet us:

"I hope you've taken an umbrella, it looks like the sky's waters are breaking!"

Each day gets its own pregnancy joke. For several weeks, I got the impression that the caretaker had feelings for me that went beyond mere guilt over my fall in the stairs. He never ceased to be courteous, but his awkwardness in my presence was palpable. Until the day Jeanne mentioned my pregnancy in front of him. I'd been sure that he must have noticed, since I'd stopped hiding it under baggy clothes. His eyes darted back and forth between Jeanne and my bump, and he remained goggle-eyed for a good minute, then burst out laughing. Since then, he's been behaving as if privy to a well-kept secret, and all ambiguity has gone.

Jeanne opens her umbrella as she steps out from the porch. I share its protection and wind my scarf around my neck. My gaze automatically falls on the shoes of someone standing on the pavement. They move up the jeans, up the jacket, and stop at the face. He smiles at me. Jeanne starts moving forward, I remain riveted to the spot.

"Hello, my angel."

Jeanne spins around and returns to stand beside me. Without knowing, she knows.

"I'm pleased to see you," Jérémy continues, moving towards me, reaching out to stroke my cheek. "I missed you so much. It took me a while to find you, but you know what they say: nothing can keep those who love each other apart. I know you think I behaved badly, but I've done a lot of thinking, and I can explain everything to you. We'll talk, okay?"

"Everything alright, Iris?" Jeanne whispers to me.

I nod my head, but my entire body is screaming the opposite. I knew this would happen, thought I was prepared, played out this moment in my mind countless times. It was easier without the leading man. I want to do just one thing: run away, disappear again, leave for a place he won't find me. I'm scared. Of him, but mainly of myself. My strength dissolves upon contact with him. My resolutions pack up and go. For three years, I was dispossessed of my convictions, my free will, by him. He pulled my strings. I was under remote control. Away from his influence, I realized to what extent. I'm terrified by the thought that he could again distort reality, make me think that my certainties are wrong. For three years, I believed him more than I believed myself. Facing him now, I'm no longer sure I've freed myself from the hold he had on me. I feel Jeanne's hand stroking my back. I can't retreat anymore. I leave the protection of the umbrella and walk towards Jérémy:

"Okay, let's go and talk."

We sit in a café. He orders two Perriers. He's wearing the sweatshirt I gave him a few days before I left. He grabs my hand:

"I've missed you so much. I was crazy with worry, at first I thought something had happened to you. It's so good to find you again. Are you pleased to see me?"

I don't reply. He smiles:

"I see you're still angry with me. I've done a lot of thinking, you know. I had the time to. We're going to be happy, the three of us. Is it a boy?"

I nod in agreement. His eyes well up:

"Louis, like my grandfather. I've cleared out the study, we can set up his room there. We're so lucky to have found each other. Soulmates are rare, Iris. I understand your anxieties as our wedding gets closer. I had my own, too, you know. But I don't have a single doubt about the fact that we're made for each other. Sometimes, when we love too much, we love badly. I'm going to help you gather up your things, and we'll go back home together. Want to finish your water first?"

I bring the glass to my lips and empty it in one go. Recently, I've often thought of Julie, a girl I met during my physio course. One day she arrived at class with stitches in her brow and a black eye. She tried to convince us she'd had an unfortunate encounter with a door, but finally confided in us. The previous day, her boyfriend had hit her. It wasn't the first time, but was one of the most violent times. She had left to live with her parents and had lodged a complaint. A while later, she went back to him. She hadn't dared tell us, we heard about it by chance.

One day, when the two of us had met up, she explained it to me. She obviously didn't love that side of him, but she did love him. He was violent, sure, but he was also thoughtful, generous, funny, attentive. He promised her he'd stop, he had therapy. I haven't seen her since our course finished, I don't know if they're still together. But I remember exactly what I thought at the time. I didn't understand her. I even passed judgment on her. From the outside, it was obvious that he would start again, that she was under his influence, that no quality could excuse his violence. From the outside, one can allow oneself just partial vision. When you share someone's life, it's harder to be so categorical. That's the danger. You see the person as a whole, with all the nuances, you can let yourself be softened up by happy memories, let qualities mitigate the unforgivable. When I look into Jérémy's eyes, I see his kiss when he's back from work, his cuddles when he knows I'm feeling blue, his loving words written on the misted-up bathroom mirror, our picnics on the beach. But the fact that all this exists doesn't stop his violence existing, too.

I put the glass down.

"I won't be coming with you, Jérémy. It's over, the wedding is canceled, I'm staying here."

He presses my hand:

"Iris, please. I know I messed up, but admit it, you left me no choice. How did you expect me to react? You're still upset over your father's death, it's completely normal. You often need help to see reason, it might seem hard, but it's for your own good. You know I'm the only one who really understands you."

Before, his thoughts would have lodged in my mind instead of my own. The distance these past months have given me allows me to see details that I couldn't when they were right under my nose. The manipulation is blatant. He reopens my wounds, tries to convince me that only he can heal them. He stripped away my self-confidence until I believed that no one but him could accept someone like me. He's an arsonist disguised as a firefighter.

"Think of the baby," he continues, squeezing my hand even tighter. "You don't realize how demanding it will all be, you'll never manage alone. And anyhow, you can't deprive him of me . . . I'm his father!"

He keeps talking, louder and louder, and yet I no longer hear him, no longer see him. My mind has flown back to La Rochelle, and the staffroom at my physiotherapy practice.

Seven months earlier

I don't know how I'm going to contain myself until tonight. He's going to be over the moon. I can't take my eyes off those two white batons. They're positive: I'm more than three weeks gone. It must have been after that Japanese restaurant a month ago. We'd argued about the man at the neighboring table. Jérémy was convinced that he was looking at me, and although I tried to tell him that he was imagining it, tried to distract him, it was all he could think about. Back home, he joined me under the shower. I was surprised by how rough he was, he wasn't usually like that.

I've been feeling tired for several days now, I even nearly drifted off during little Timeo's therapy. But mainly, my period didn't come. I confided in my colleague Coralie, part of me was hoping. During the lunch break, she went off to buy me some pregnancy tests. I couldn't believe it: falling pregnant while taking the Pill can happen, but only very rarely.

I don't know how to break the news to Jérémy. He doesn't like surprises, but I'm determined to make the occasion unforgettable. Last week, he again cried watching a birth scene on TV. When I see him with his friend Fred's little girl, I know he'll make a wonderful father. He can be demanding sometimes, but it's always justified.

"With or Without You," Jérémy's ringtone on my phone, starts up, as it does several times a day. I answer every time, busy or

not. Once, I'd forgotten my phone in the office while with a patient, and there were thirty-two missed calls, and almost as many anxious messages. I try to sound casual, so he suspects nothing. I want to tell him face to face. I want to see his expression when he learns he'll soon be a daddy.

The conversation lasts two minutes, the rest of the day an eternity. I've never been in such a hurry to get home. Jérémy arrives half an hour after me. He's smiling, comes over to kiss me. It's now the weekend, tomorrow we're off to visit some caves in the Dordogne. I take a few steps back and lift up my T-shirt. On my tummy I've written, in felt-pen, "Baby loading . . ."

"You're going to be a daddy, sweetheart."

He smiles even more:

"What do you mean?"

"Well, it seems your sperm fertilized my ovum, and we'll soon be the parents of a little mite that cries and poos."

He laughs, thinks it's a joke. I take the test sticks out of the back pocket of my jeans.

"Are you having me on?"

His smile has gone, his voice is ice-cold. My joy freezes up. He realizes, softens, takes me in his arms.

"We're great together, my angel. Just you and me. A child would push us apart, that's for sure. We love each other too much."

My head is pressed between his chest and his arms. I squeeze the sticks in my hand.

"I thought you'd be pleased."

He suddenly pushes me away, I almost trip on the carpet.

"Don't try to make me feel guilty," he says, coldly. "We've talked about this several times, I've never said I wanted one now. Maybe one day, we'll see. I thought that was clear between us."

"I hadn't understood that, no."

"Of course, you're always trying to rewrite history! If you were a little attentive to others, you'd never have played that nasty trick on me. You should have sorted the problem out without telling me about it. The weekend is ruined."

He walks around me and heads for the bathroom. I'm paralyzed, incapable of knowing how to react. I have just one certainty: I loved this child the moment a blue line made it exist in my mind.

I'm preparing supper when he emerges from the shower. He's got dressed.

"Shall we eat out somewhere?" he asks me.

"I'm not hungry."

"Fuck's sake, Iris, you're not going to make a meal of this! Am I not enough for you, is that it?"

I carry on peeling the cucumber, I don't answer. He walks the few steps between us and sticks his face right up against mine.

"Answer!" he roars. "Am I not enough for you?"

I choke back my tears:

"You are, that's got nothing to do with it."

"It's got everything to do with it! I want us to stay just us, you can't impose a baby on me. You must have forgotten your Pill, you just should have been careful. Now, it's for you to sort it out."

"What do you mean?"

"'What do you mean?'" he repeats, mimicking me. "Do you want a diagram? You sort out the problem, I don't want to hear a thing about it. I don't even know if it's mine."

I've learnt not to respond, so as not to his stoke his rage. Sometimes, it works. But sometimes he takes my silence for disdain, and that's worse.

He grabs my shoulder and pulls on it, violently. I'm propelled far from the worktop. In a protective reflex, I place both hands on my stomach. That drives him crazy. I barely have time to see his arm going up before a powerful slap stuns me. My ear is throbbing, I put a hand to my cheek, his chance to punch me in the stomach. I hear a howl—mine—and manage to run away to the bedroom. Crouching behind the bed, I try to hear his steps through the pounding of my heart and the ringing in my ear. He joins me only much later, when it's time for bed. Facing the wall, I pretend to sleep.

"I didn't mean to do that, my angel. You made me fly off the handle. I won't do it again, promise. Are you angry with me?"
I don't respond.
"Iris, are you angry with me?" he asks, louder.
"No," I whisper, trying to control my trembling.
He lies down against me, his breath on the nape of my neck, his hands on my breasts, then moving down, down to my stomach.
"I'll let you sort it out, okay?" he murmurs.
No response.
"Iris, okay?"
"Okay."
I don't sleep a wink all night. Each second is an ordeal. My brain is in turmoil, I keep changing my mind. Stay with him and forgive him? Try to persuade him? Return to my parents? Go somewhere else? Where? Cancel the wedding? Do without him? Give up my life? Give up my baby? And what if he finds me? And what if he's right?
Early in the morning, he kisses me before going for his jog. "See you later, my angel, I'll bring back the croissants." I wait for the door to slam, then, from the window, watch him set off. I stuff whatever comes to hand into the green suitcase. I leave a note. "I'd rather do without you than the baby. Don't look for me." My heart is about to explode as I leave the house. I start the car and drive off without knowing where to go.

"Come on, my angel, be reasonable," Jérémy says, grabbing my other hand. "You want apologies? Fine, I apologize. I made a clumsy move, you caught me off guard and I panicked. Is that worth throwing everything away for? Is that worth making me suffer so much? I could do something really stupid, you know. And just think about those invited to the wedding. Think about your mother. I know you love me, I can see it in your eyes. We're stronger than that. Let's go home and build our family."

I remove my hands from his hold and look him straight in the eye.

"I won't come back. It wasn't a clumsy move, it was violence.

The climax of an abusive relationship. I'm not going to argue about it, I know you'll always manage to turn the situation around and convince yourself that you're the victim. Carrying a child has opened my eyes. What I accepted for myself I refuse to accept for him. I'm going to rebuild myself, I've already made a good start. I'm not afraid of you anymore, and you no longer have a hold on me. You don't love me, Jérémy, and I didn't love the person I'd become with you. I don't want to see you anymore. If you come near me again, I'll lodge a formal complaint. I went to A&E the day after your blows, to check the baby was alright. I have the proof. Stay well away from us."

I've never shaken so much. I pick up my bag and coat, and I leave the café. On the pavement, Jeanne makes room for me under her umbrella.

71
JEANNE

This journey to visit Pierre was the most emotional one Jeanne had ever made. Her night had been restless. What she was about to do was of particular importance to her.

She tried to avoid thinking by focusing on the pedestrians, cars, and store windows going past on the other side of the bus window. When that stopped working, she reflected on the events of recent days. She had been alarmed by the look in Iris's eyes when she had recognized her ex. After the two had talked, Iris had told her roommates her story, the broad outlines of which Jeanne had guessed. Théo had suggested going to sort Jérémy out, arguing that his three months of karate gave him a definite advantage over the enemy. He did, however, seem relieved when Iris wouldn't hear of it. That evening, with every secret shared, Jeanne, Iris and Théo had officially turned from roommates into friends.

Jeanne approached Pierre gently. Her hands were shaking more than usual. She stroked his photo with unchanged emotion. She remembered how hard she had found choosing it. She had dug out all the albums, and each photo had revived her memory of the moment it captured. Should she go for a formal pose, which barely looked like him, or a more natural, but less conventional, one? The wedding portrait or the sunset at Saint-Jean-de-Luz? In a suit or in jeans? He had been all that, no single image could represent him as she knew him.

"Hello, my love," she murmured. "I haven't come alone today."

She beckoned to her two companions, who had hung back until then. They joined her.

"Meet Iris and Théo. Iris, Théo, meet Pierre."

Iris greeted the headstone out loud, whereas Théo managed

an awkward bow. For the occasion, without Jeanne asking, he had put on the shirt she had tried to get him to wear for his date at Leïla's, and slipped the bowtie around his neck. Jeanne had been careful not to laugh, touched as she was by the gesture. Iris, on the other hand, had been in hysterics.

"They're part of my life. I wish you could have known them differently, not just by what I tell you. Iris is a young woman of amazing strength and profound generosity. She's carrying one very lucky baby. Théo is young man of great sensitivity and boundless courage. It's you who put them on my path, I'm sure of it. I needed at least these two to get over you."

With the back of his hand, Théo brushed away some non-existent dust attacking his eyes. Iris blew her nose. When Jeanne changed the subject, they went to sit on the bench, to give her some privacy.

"I want to be cremated," Théo said, suddenly. "I don't want to oblige people to come and weep over my grave. My mother used to feel terribly guilty if she hadn't been to the cemetery for a while. I'd prefer people to think about me when they feel like it."

"Well, I'd prefer not to die," Iris joked.

"Oh yeah, that would be cool, too. But if you don't mind me saying, you'll have to learn how to use the stairs for that."

Jeanne stayed just as long as she usually did. Iris and Théo had ample time to watch the coming and going of cemetery visitors. The grief-stricken, the resigned, the rushed, the contemplative, the curious, the damaged; single people, couples, groups, great-granddaughters, grandsons, orphans, widows, mothers, grandfathers, sisters, cousins, friends.

"We can go!" Jeanne announced, setting off.

Iris and Théo followed her, but then he turned back and went over to Pierre's grave. Watched by the two women, but too far to be heard by them, he whispered:

"I'm not sold on all this stuff, but if it really is you who put me on your wife's path, I thank you. Because, by doing so, you put her on my path."

Théo

I knew my car would be destroyed. I received a letter informing me that the pound wouldn't keep it for more than thirty days. It specified that I could recover my personal effects by paying the charges and proving that it really was my car. That's what I cared about most. I'd put a little dough aside every month and, seeing as I now had two hundred euros, I thought that would do, so turned up at the Montreuil pound. When the guy gave me the bill, I instantly saw that there'd been a mistake.

"You've put one zero too many," I told him.

"You're a smart alec, you are," he told me.

There wasn't one zero too many, and no way of paying in installments, either. I left my mother's little notes, her Barry White LP, and the only photo of my brother with me, there, and when I win the lottery, I'll go and get them back. I don't need objects to keep my memories alive, but those things I am attached to. I leave the pound with my head in the past. It's time, now, to immerse myself in it.

It's seven o'clock. I walk as far as the house with blue shutters. It often features in the imaginary life I return to every night once I'm in bed. Behind my closed eyelids, I've pressed that doorbell dozens of times. But I've never trembled as much as now, doing it for real. I feel like running away while I still can, but the door opens. A man comes out. He must be close to fifty now. He looks at me, waiting for me to try to flog him a veranda.

"Marc?"

"Yes. And you are?"

I still have the choice. There's the fear of doing something stupid, of regretting, of coming at the wrong time, of sidetracking fate.

"I'm Théo. Laure's son."

He walks down the two steps and joins me. I can't tell whether he's pleased or not. I just stand there, legs like jelly, heart in mouth.

He grasps me by the neck and draws me to him. He holds me tight, and it all comes back: his smell of leather and cigarettes, his prickly cheeks, his laugh, the stories he'd read me at night, the drawings he'd teach me to do, the exercises he'd help me to tackle. Not my father, but the closest thing to it.

"Jeez, Théo. I knew you'd come one day. You kept my address, hey?"

Impossible to speak, so I answer with my head. He reopens the door and ushers me into the house with blue shutters. It doesn't look like the one in my imaginary world, it's smaller, there's more clutter, but it has the advantage of being real. A little girl runs up. When she sees me, she clings to her father's legs.

"Mia, are you going to say hi to Théo? He's your brother's brother, so he's kinda your brother, too."

"I have a new brother?"

We reach the sitting room, a woman is seated on the sofa, she looks at me, fixedly. Marc moves over to her, I follow him, not knowing what to expect.

"This is Théo, Laure's son."

"That's what I thought," she says, smiling at me. "Well, I'm Ludivine. I'm pleased to meet you."

It's too good—even in my head I didn't dare go this far. Marc wants to know what I do, where I live, he asks nothing about my mother, but I tell him about the accident, because I've never been able to share it with anyone who loved her.

"I'm so sorry. I didn't know. Five years ago, you say? Is that why you stopped replying to my letters?"

I say yes, but the truth is that I stopped replying because I stopped reading them. When I'd see those photos of them, it would remind me too much of what I'd had, and that I no longer had.

"She wasn't a bad woman, your mother. She wasn't cut out for this world."

Ludivine doesn't bite me, Mia asks me loads of questions, a tabby cat rubs itself against my calves, I start to relax, but the most important thing is missing.

"He's not here?"

"Your brother? He's doing his homework in his room! Come, we'll go and see him."

He makes me go up the stairs first. The whole family is behind me. I feel as if I'm about to accomplish something big, and that is, indeed, what's about to happen.

There's a no-entry sign on the door. A real one, not a sticker. I laugh inside because, with Gérard and Ahmed, I'd swiped one from the crossroads near the townhall. We didn't even get as far as our room, we were busted by the youth workers, and had to take it back to where we'd found it.

Marc reaches in front of me, presses the door handle, and indicates for me to go in. The room is dark, but for some string lights and the desk lamp. My brother turns around upon hearing the door. On his face, surprise:

"Théo? What are you doing here? There's no karate this evening!"

"Hi, Sam."

73
IRIS

Since my conversation with Jérémy, my bump has doubled in size. Jeanne reckons I'm finally allowing myself to be pregnant, I reckon it's mainly calories that I'm allowing myself. In a little over a month, I'll be gobbling up chubby thighs. In the meantime, I do justice to Théo's pastries—he deems it his duty to make me one a day. Jeanne, out of mere solidarity, joins me in my tastings. He's talented, the little twit, so, occasionally, I let him mimic my penguin-like waddle.

Naively, I thought my showdown with Jérémy would suffice. He's phoned me up to two hundred times a day, inundated me with messages, sometimes imploring, sometimes threatening. I've replied to none of them. One morning, as I was setting off to walk Boudine, I found myself face to face with him on the stairs. He tried to drag me down by force, gripping my arm, his fingers digging into my skin. I resisted, I struggled, he shoved me against the wall, telling me to shut my mouth. I did so until the ground floor, when I started screaming outside Victor's window. He'd barely stuck his head out before Jérémy cleared off.

Jeanne went with me to the police station. The policewoman who recorded my complaint told me he would soon be summoned. For several days, I heard nothing from him. This wasn't reassuring. I prefer it when he makes a noise, then I know where he's coming from. He finally got in touch this morning, with a text message.

"Iris, I'm sorry it's got to this, but I can't put up with your behavior any longer. I'm ending our relationship. There's no point replying to this, or trying to contact me, I won't change my mind. I'll take care of canceling the wedding. I'll recoup the money already spent by selling the things you left at my place. Don't bother asking me for maintenance, you can't force me to recognize the child legally. You can just explain to him what a wonderful mother you are. I gave you everything, but you always have to have more. Good luck to the next guy. Jérémy."

Tentatively, I allowed myself to feel relief. I can't entirely believe it. I've never known Jérémy give up on anything. Not even a book once started. He keeps going to the end, as a matter of principal. So, his future wife . . .

Whether he disappears or not, I won't get rid of him that easily. Even absent, he's present. His shadow will hover over me for a long time. I'll continue to turn around in the street, jump when I hear a voice, think someone else is him. But time is my ally. Each day, I get further away from him and closer to myself.

It's time I clear up a minor issue. I sit on the edge of my bed and make the call.

"Mom, it's me."

I can now give her the truth without worrying her. I tell her about the vicious words, the humiliations, the reproaches, the violence. The fear, the shame, the isolation. I leave out the sordid details, but without giving her a chance to find excuses for Jérémy. When I've finished, her sobs are her reply.

"I never imagined . . . " she finally murmurs, catching her breath back. "He doesn't seem . . . he's so . . . well, you know, I'd never have thought that of him. I'm so sorry, darling, you must have felt so alone."

She starts crying again, I reassure her: she saw what I wanted her to see, she has nothing to feel guilty about.

"Why didn't you talk to me about it? Believe me, I'd have pushed you to leave him much sooner, if I'd known."

"Mom, it's more complicated than that, you know."

"Yes, yes, no doubt, but all the same. One mustn't wait, at the first warning sign, one must go. I don't understand those women who stay with violent men. They share some responsib . . . "

She doesn't finish her sentence. That sentence I've heard so often, for so long. From my own mouth, sometimes. That sentence that reverses the roles, reduces the responsibility of the guilty party and accuses the victim. That sentence that lets domestically abused women think they must deserve it a bit, in the end, since they haven't left. Maybe my mother will understand, now that that sentence is about her daughter. Because human beings are like that, unfortunately: they only really understand things when personally confronted with them.

Fear. Love. Control. Guilt. The children. Loneliness. Lack of means. Nowhere to go. There are as many reasons as there are situations. A victim is never responsible.

After a few seconds of silence, my mother continues:

"I'm going to throw away the vase he gave me. I want nothing more from him. He'd better not dare come back here, I'll give him a welcome he won't forget!"

"There's something else, Mom."

"Oh."

"I can't tell you why I stayed, but I can tell you why I left."

When I join Jeanne and Théo in the sitting room, after telling my mother she is soon to be a grandma—and receiving her joy and advice in return—a rum baba awaits me.

"It's alcohol-free rum!" Théo reassures me.

Jeanne grabs her teaspoon:

"I do hope mine's got alcohol in it."

74
JEANNE

Jeanne had held back her tears for most of her life. She hadn't just hidden them from others, even when alone, with no one to judge her, she had swallowed them. It's what she had been taught to do, and she had obeyed with a rigor that demanded respect. At Pierre's funeral, she'd been determined to remain dignified, while still wondering why that term meant an absence of tears. As if crying was undignified, as if pain was vulgar.

The force of her grief had burst the dam. The first time, she'd feared she'd never stop crying. Her whole body had joined in the outpouring: her eyes, her mouth, her throat, her diaphragm, her stomach, her hands. She had felt like an animal, wild, and had ended up drained, but surprisingly soothed. This unexpected discovery had encouraged her to let herself go again, as soon as she felt the need. Jeanne now cried morning, noon, and night, depending on her self-prescribed needs. Her floods of tears watered down missing Pierre, Louise's absence, her parents' death, her empty womb.

Crying consoled. She wished she'd known that sooner. She couldn't fathom why shame was attached to such a liberating act. So, when Iris wept when saying that her child wouldn't know his grandfather, Jeanne didn't attempt to stem her tears. On the contrary, she took her in her arms and encouraged her to let her grief pour out.

She was very fond of her, this dear girl. Iris quite often reminded her of herself, with her defensive layers and excessive respect for conventions. She enjoyed mornings in her company, sewing while chatting about everything and nothing, and, implicitly, themselves. It was one of her newfound routines.

"Good grief!" Jeanne exclaimed, looking up from the sleepsuit she was making. "I hadn't noticed the time, I'm running awfully late."

She grabbed her bag, put on her coat and shoes, and left the apartment like a whirlwind. She was preoccupied for the entire journey. It was unthinkable. She had, purely and simply, forgotten her appointment with Pierre.

When she finally reached him, she couldn't help but apologize profusely.

"I was totally absorbed in my sewing. It's very detailed work, I'm doing the broderie anglaise by hand. I didn't notice the hours fly by. It's the first time this has happened to me, I can't get over it."

Jeanne wiped the plaque with care. The previous day's rain had left traces on it. As she went to the tap to get fresh water for the flowers, she noticed something which, until then, had passed her by. It made her drop the vase. With a hand over her mouth, she approached the neighboring grave. It had always been decked with flowers, what with Simone always replacing any bouquets or arrangements at the first sign of wilting, but never to this extent. The sprays and wreaths covered the stone entirely. New plaques also seemed to have appeared. She went closer to confirm what she feared. Simone Mignot was now spending all of her time with her husband.

Jeanne felt unexpectedly sad about this woman whom, really, she barely knew, but with whom she shared a good deal. She forgot about the vase and conventions.

"Simone is dead," she said, breathlessly, returning to Pierre. "I thought she'd returned to life, released from her shackles, but I got it totally wrong. She's died after not living. I keep thinking of what she said to me here, on New Year's Day. 'Life is to be found on the other side of that gate.' It's no coincidence, my love. Today, I forgot our appointment because I was busy living. I know what you'd say to me, if you saw me coming here every day."

She paused, her gaze fixed on the empty bench, and then took a deep breath:

"The charity I donate my creations to suggested I give sewing lessons to women who are in a precarious situation. I declined, as it would have kept me from visiting you on two afternoons a week. But actually, I'm going to say yes. I'll still come and bother you often, don't think I'm going to change completely. But our meetings won't necessarily take place here anymore. You are with me every second, in every breath I take."

Jeanne stroked the photo of her beloved Pierre.

"Come, my love, I'm taking you to the other side of that gate."

75
THÉO

I was in two minds about dropping karate. I only signed up in the hope of getting to know my brother, and never really got into it, but it's still extra time spent with Sam.

I can't stop replaying the scene of our reunion in my mind. When, for once, reality is better than my imaginary life, I'm not going to deprive myself. He was sitting at his desk, pretending to do his homework. It was his father who explained who I am, my voice having deserted me. He has no early memory of me, unsurprisingly since he must have been three when he last saw me, but, apparently, he's often heard people speak about me. If I'd known there was somewhere on the planet where I existed for someone, I wouldn't have delayed coming.

Marc was filming the scene. Sam's little sister went over to her brother for a hug. He wasn't very happy about the karate trick.

"I don't see why you lied."

"I didn't know how you'd react. I didn't even know if you knew you had a brother."

"Dad was sure you'd come here one day. I had no idea. Mustn't count your chickens before they're fucking hatched."

"Sam, you really must stop using that language!" said Marc, halting filming.

The kid looked at me, laughing, and I couldn't stop myself from doing the same. Our mother would have probably called him "my little clown," too.

They wanted me to stay for supper, but I chose to go home. I was already overflowing with emotions.

I've received two texts from Marc since then, but no news from Sam.

At the start of the karate class, waiting for Sam to turn up, I felt like when you're seeing a girl again after a first kiss. Wondering if he would shake my hand, give me a hug, or snub me. He said hi from a distance, and hasn't said a word to me since. I caught the odd sidelong glance, but that's all. As soon as the class is over, I don't even get changed, I stay in my kimono, put on my sneakers and jacket, and rush off. I've almost reached the metro station when I hear the sound of a bicycle behind me.

"Théo! Will you walk me home?"

I shrug, to seem blasé, but my brain is doing somersaults. He pushes his bike, I walk beside him and refrain from telling him that the first time we'd done that, it was me who'd let down his tires.

"You were off like a shot," he says.

"I start work early tomorrow."

"Lucky you! My dad told me you're a baker. I can't wait to work, but that won't be any time soon. I hate school, especially math. Right now, we're doing division, it drives me crazy."

"What do you want to do, later on?"

"I dream of working in one of those little cabins, where you pay, at gas stations. My dad says that's not a profession, but you get to see loads of people and you're sitting down, it must be wick-ed. Otherwise, a rock-climbing or karate teacher. Any news from Mom?"

The question throws me.

"Your father didn't explain to you?"

"She had an accident, is that it? Do you visit her often?"

"Once a month. Would you like us to ask your father if you can come, too?"

He stops to retie his shoelace, while I hold his bike.

"Dunno," he replies. "My real mother is Ludivine. The other one abandoned me."

I don't react. Some things become clearer not with explanations, but with time. One day, perhaps, Sam will know that it was more complicated than that. It's not us she abandoned, it's herself. She was trapped in a relationship that overpowered her. One day, I'll make him read what she wrote when I was little, the text I stuck on the wall in her room. They'd found it in her wallet after the accident. She'd called it, "Paint on the mouth."

We arrive at the house with blue shutters. Sam high-fives me and asks if we'll meet up again before the next karate class. I suggest we go see a movie at the weekend, he agrees, and once he's opened the door, he suddenly says:

"You took a long time coming, but I'm happy to have a brother."

Paint on the mouth

"Why've you put paint on your mouth?"

I stroke your curls, praying that you're not really expecting an answer. Which one could I possibly give you? "My darling, Mommy is about to do the stupidest thing in her life, so she thought a touch of lipstick might help her feel less ugly, that's all, so, sweet dreams now."

I tuck you and Teddy in. You've put on odd socks again, the bear cubs and the stars. You're so little.

I feel like lying down beside you, burying my nose in your hair and hugging you tight, but it's already too late. I can't back out anymore. I kiss you one last time and close the door of your cocoon. A few meters away from you, in the kitchen so you don't see him, my first love awaits me.

Five years we've not seen each other. I did glimpse him a few times, but managed to ignore him. I'd promised that to your father.

My hand is on the doorknob, paralyzed with guilt. How can I invite him to my home, our home, after all the harm he did me? I already know he won't leave. He disgusts me as much as he attracts me. I loathe him as much as I love him.

I wasn't even twenty when I first met him. It was at a party, everyone was having fun, and I, as usual, was held back by my shyness. I felt like I was transparent.

Until I saw him.

His look, his blondness, his smell. His popularity. I attached myself to him and didn't leave him all evening. I admitted my angst to him, he reassured me, consoled me. He even got me to dance. The others didn't matter anymore.

We got together again the following day. I'd never felt so beautiful, so funny, so strong. With him, everything was possible. He made me the girl I'd always dreamed of being.

I was so happy.

It didn't last.

Everyone loved him, except my parents. They forbade me from seeing him, but I couldn't do without him. I started to lie, to find pretexts to meet up with him. I'd spend entire nights outside, or get him into the house when everyone was asleep. One night, I woke up my mother with my giggling. I didn't hear her coming in, she caught the two of us in my room. She started screaming and threw him down the stairs. I left with him.

Things went downhill from then on. When I met your father, I was a wreck after years of being controlled. He rescued me from that relationship, patched me up with his love and patience. We found a house, I found a job, we got married. I learned to love this simple happiness, even if I couldn't quite forget the other guy. How often did I almost cave in, how often did I struggle not to go back to him?

And then you arrived, with your long eyelashes that spread happiness and your smiles that wiped away ugliness. The past really became just that on the day you were born. Forgotten, the violence, the betrayals, the lies. Life was giving me a chance. Death took it back from me.

Since your father passed away, I've been trying to keep going, I promise you, my darling. I focus as hard as I can on my promises and your future, but the other guy is there, in my mind, in my flesh, in my dreams. My head pushes him away, but my body yearns for him.

Just once. One little time.

I open the kitchen door. He's there, in front of me. He hasn't changed.

It's so good to smell him so close.

With a final jolt, I try to remember how he alienated me from my loved ones, made me abandon my studies, made me ill. But his smell. God, that smell.

I take one step towards him.

My heart is beating in my temples, I'm not thinking anymore. I reach out, he's there. I touch him, caress him. I've missed him so much. I close my eyes and move my lips closer.

Just once. One little time.

I don't know what time it is when the door to your room opens. I don't even know what day it is anymore. Or why I'm laughing out loud. I don't see you straight away. I don't hear your little odd socks approaching me. Sprawled on the sofa, I barely turn my head when your voice reaches me.

"Are you okay, Mommy? What are you doing on the sofa? Who are you talking to? The paint on your mouth is all smudged . . ."

Everything's fine, nothing's serious. I'm strong, I'm funny, I'm beautiful. Nothing can happen to us.

"Go back to bed, darling. Mommy's spending the evening with an old friend."

And I laugh again, before bringing the glass mouth of my first love to my lips.

76
IRIS

Jeanne doesn't want to come with me on my daily walk.

"It's Sunday, I've got better things to do," she declares.

Better, it would seem, is being engrossed in a TV report on manatees, alongside Théo. I wonder if I should read something into this, since these creatures' way of moving reminds me strangely of my own.

It takes me forever to get down the three flights of stairs. I'm seriously considering installing a pulley system to assist my ailing ligaments. Unlike his mistress, Boudine had shown some enthusiasm, but that promptly disappears when faced with my slowness.

Pregnancy has heightened my emotions, I'm an exaggerated version of myself. I swing from moaning to marveling, laughter to tears. Every day, I love my son more, I imagine his face, I talk to him, I sniff his clothes. I've bought a few, but most have been made by Jeanne. I so can't wait to see him in them. My impatience has, however, been tempered by the latest ultrasound. If the estimated birth weight is to be believed, my son, like Attila, is going to destroy everything in his path.

Jérémy wouldn't be able to put up with me pregnant.

As I feared, the respite from him was short-lived. Barely a few hours after his break-up message, he sent another message: "My angel, give us a chance, we'll make the effort needed. Don't do this to me. I love you." I didn't reply to it, or to those that followed. I was hoping that my registering a formal complaint would make him see reason, but that's clearly not the case. He's determined to be the decision-maker. He'll lose interest in me when it suits him, maybe in favor of someone new, maybe just from weariness. In the meantime, I'm staying on my guard. In the end, the situation hasn't evolved since I left La Rochelle. And yet everything is different: I'm no longer alone.

Boudine and I get home nearly two hours later, of which one-and-a-half were spent on the stairs. Why on earth didn't I pick a building with an elevator. This is all going to end badly. I can picture the headlines: "World record: pregnant woman— or is it a manatee?—takes three days, four hours and fifty-six minutes to leave apartment. Crane brought in as back-up."

Jeanne and Théo haven't budged a millimeter. This is suspicious, if Victor's claim to have come across them in the hall during my absence is to be believed.

"Did you go downstairs?" I ask.

"Absolutely not!" Jeanne is quick to reply.

"Why?" Théo asks.

"Because Victor saw the two of you downstairs."

"What a fink," Jeanne mutters.

She stands up and indicates for me to follow her, with Théo hot on her heels, and Boudine hot on his.

"Close your eyes, no cheating!" she orders me, outside my bedroom door.

I hear creaking, Boudine's claws on the parquet, the curtain being drawn, a chuckle, and: "Ta-dah!" I open my eyes. The little table, which I never used, has disappeared. Instead, a sea-green cradle takes pride of place.

"It looks like . . . "

I don't finish my sentence, for fear of hurting Jeanne. She finishes it for me:

"It *is* the cradle that was in the cellar. Théo and I repainted it, I noticed that you like green . . . "

"Jeanne, it's . . . I don't know what to say. It's wonderful."

Théo puts his hands to his mouth to mimic the sound of a microphone:

"Releasing of tears, three, two, one . . . "

I try to dam them, to prove him wrong, but my tear ducts are on his side. Jeanne gives me a hug.

"I'm happy it's finally being used," she murmurs. "I so dreamt of seeing a baby in it."

"You're the pits, you two," says Théo. "I've spent my life building up my defenses, and then you come along and just blow them to bits."

77
JEANNE

Jeanne was reading the letter she'd just found in the mailbox when Iris joined her in the sitting room.

"I think I'm having contractions."

Since forever, Jeanne had claimed to be totally unflappable. Time and again, she had assured Pierre that, in an emergency, she'd be able to think calmly and make rational decisions. So, faced with her young friend's sudden announcement, she was able to react sensibly and methodically:

"Oh, shit."

"It can't be, it's too early," Iris reassured her. "It must be a false alarm. It'll be fine."

Her demonstration of this was to double up and let out a long groan. Jeanne jumped to her feet.

"Let's go to the hospital."

"Wait, there's no rush. The midwife told me that you could get contractions several weeks before the birth, it's fine OWWWWW SHIIIIIT THAT HUUUUURTS!"

Jeanne froze for a few seconds, before pulling herself together and dragging Iris off to the hospital.

By the second floor, the flaw in her plan was clear: Iris was going down one step per contraction. At this rate, by the time they reached the ground floor, the child would be three years old. She took out her phone and rang Victor. He was there in seconds, and carried the future mom and her cargo down the stairs.

Fortunately, the hospital was just two streets away. Victor escorted the two women. Iris had to stop several times, leaning on Jeanne, who almost keeled over at every groan.

Jeanne had never been so closely involved in a pregnancy, let alone a delivery. But that wasn't the only reason she felt emotional. She had feelings for Iris and Théo that she'd never known before. She'd never presume to say she loved them as if they were her own children. She loved them, period, and that was reason enough to worry about them.

"It might be Théo's tarte Tatin," Iris gasped, between contractions. "It tasted weird, I didn't dare say anything."

"Iris, you're going to give birth," Jeanne responded, firmly.

Iris denied this, before being reduced to silence by another wave of pain.

At the hospital reception, Jeanne explained why they had come, and managed to find all the required documents in Iris's bag. When Iris was being taken to an examination room, Jeanne set off for the waiting room.

"Jeanne, do you mind coming with me?"

She didn't need persuading. At first, she parked herself in a corner of the room so as not to get in the way of the medical team. She was impressed by what she saw. A man placed two straps around Iris's belly and slipped sensors beneath them. Numbers appeared on the screen of a machine.

"That, there, is your baby's heartbeat rate. And there, the intensity of contractions. Tell us when you feel one coming."

A woman was examining Iris internally. Instinctively, Jeanne went up to her friend and stroked her forehead.

"It's going to be fine."

"I'm wasting their time," she replied.

A grimace distorted her face, and directly, Jeanne saw her belly tauten until it was hard. The number on the screen skyrocketed. The midwife pulled off her gloves and moved towards Iris.

"Labor has begun. When you leave here, you'll have your baby with you."

Iris laughed and cried all at once. Jeanne held her hand and stroked it with her thumb.

"You will stay with me, won't you?"

Jeanne nodded, then went over to the first person in a pink gown she saw and asked if there was somewhere she could lie down for a few minutes before she passed out.

Théo

Nathalie is in a foul mood. You have to know her well to realize that because her face is forever in a foul mood, but now, as well as sighing every ten seconds, she's grunting. Or rather, she sounds like a lawn mower refusing to start. It's because of Leïla. She dared to challenge Nathalie in front of a customer. He'd asked for a baguette that was not too crisp, Nathalie had given him a dark brown one, and Leïla had suggested another paler one. And Nathalie has been going on about it ever since.

"You cannot make me lose face in front of the customers. Who do you think you are? You don't have my experience, just in case you've forgotten. How does it make me look?"

I have an answer to this last question, but I'm not sure she'd like it. Whenever she can, Leïla gestures at me to convey her woe, or to mimic Nathalie. I laugh, but I'm scared Nathalie will see her. Though I'm sure she's already caught us at it . . .

Whenever Leïla and I cross paths, we manage to touch each other. We can't help it, I've never felt like this, I have to see her, feel her, hear her. Anyhow, she walked behind me while I was making the crème anglaise, and took the chance to stroke my butt. We heard such a freaky scream, it made us both jump.

"What's that?" Nathalie asked, pointing at my butt.

"That?" I replied. "I believe it's my ass."

"Don't play it clever with me, you two, I know exactly what you're up to. Leïla, why did you touch his buttocks?"

"I didn't mean to, I slipped and grabbed hold of what I could."

It was hard not to laugh.

"Are you a couple?"

"No way," we replied, in unison.

"Watch out, both of you! I've got my eye on you. No love stories here, this isn't *The Dating Game*."

I didn't know what she was on about, but I said nothing. We got back to work, hoping we'd convinced her, but I still have my doubts.

My phone vibrates in my pocket. I hide to answer it, otherwise she'll give me another truckload of shit. It's Jeanne. I shut myself away in the restroom and speak in a whisper.

"Jeanne, everything okay?"

"Iris is having her baby."

I have to wait three hours before I can go there. Nathalie would refuse for me to leave early, I don't even ask. As soon as I'm done, I rush to the hospital. A woman asks if I'm a relation of Iris.

"I'm her son."

She takes me into a room.

"It may take a very long time," she says. "Would you like a TV?"

"No, thanks. I'll be fine."

I instantly regret it. My phone battery is dying, and my imaginary world is hard to access when I'm stressed. All I can do is read the hospital rules and the posters on breastfeeding and skin-to-skin contact. I message Leïla about it, to make her laugh. She turns up an hour later with a charger and some sandwiches.

I have a knot in my stomach, I can't face food, but I force myself because I'm so touched by her gesture. She must sense it:

"Are you scared?"

"A bit."

"You like her a lot, don't you?"

I consider for a few moments, because it's a novelty, unfamiliar, not yet logged in my internal database, and I reply:

"Yes, a lot. Jeanne and Iris, they're my family."

Iris

Gabin is sleeping, curled up on my chest.

Gabin Dominique. My father's name as a middle name.

I didn't know what to expect. Some speak of an instant love, others need time before really meeting their child. I'd prepared myself for either possibility. It was an explosion. My heart expanded so there was space for him inside. When the midwife laid him on me, his eyes looked deep into mine, and in them I saw all that he entrusted to me, all that awaited us. I feel complete. I didn't know I was lacking something until he came and filled the gap.

The porter pushes my bed along the corridors. I'm going up to the ward. Jeanne walks alongside us. She stayed for the nine hours of labor, holding my hand, encouraging me, reassuring me, turning a deaf ear when I cursed the whole world. She updated my mother, who hit the road as soon as she knew. She'll be here late morning.

The door opens, Théo is asleep in the armchair. He jumps when he hears us.

"I wasn't asleep!" he protests, his eyes half-shut. "Leïla left, she had to rest, oh my god, he's so small!"

"Tell that to my perineum."

He laughs. I gently turn Gabin around, Théo leans closer to study his face.

"He's beautiful. Don't know who he gets that from."

Jeanne chuckles, then gives me a questioning glance to check if she can touch him.

"Would you like to hold him?" I ask.

"Not on your life!" exclaims Théo, backing away. "I don't touch on the first date."

"I was talking to Jeanne."

"I'd like that," she murmurs, her eyes shining.

Our four hands lift him up, and after a few dicey moves, she manages to prop Gabin up in the crook of her left arm. She gently strokes his cheek, holds his tiny fingers, kisses his forehead, and I just watch them, wondering how much a heart can swell without bursting.

"Got to go to work," says Théo, checking the time on his phone. "I'll come by to see you this evening, if you're not too tired."

"I'm coming with you," says Jeanne, settling Gabin back with me. "Iris needs to rest, and I do, too."

She leans over to plant a kiss on my forehead, then steps back and looks deep into my eyes.

"Thank you, my dear. That was one of the most beautiful moments of my life."

I don't need to reply, my eyes tell her exactly how I feel.

I find myself alone with my son. His stomach rises to the rhythm of his breathing. Sometimes, a little moan escapes from his mouth. He's in a white velour sleepsuit with matching hat, both made by Jeanne. I can't take my eyes off him. I already know that I'll never tire of this sight. This immensely small life is making me live immensely big things.

I'm going to savor these hours, one to one with my son. I'm going to gorge myself on his smell, his tears, his sudden starts. And then I'll return to that apartment where, by chance, one day last year, I ended up with two perfect strangers I had no desire to know better. That apartment that was only supposed to be a temporary refuge, and became my home. Those perfect strangers who were only supposed to be provisional roommates, and became my friends. I'm going to resume my life, the one they're now a part of.

There are still many uncertainties. I don't know if I'll finally find my own apartment, if I'll return to my physiotherapy work, if I'll remain in Paris. Tomorrow is another life. But there is one thing I'm sure about. Some bonds take decades to forge, others rapidly become unbreakable. They're certainties. Jeanne and Théo are my certainties. Whatever happens, we'll still have that.

Epilogue

15 June

Jeanne sank her feet into the pool of sunlight bathing her floorboards. A year earlier, to the day, she had done just this, appreciated this same warmth, felt this same serenity, just before her world was turned upside down. She stood for a long time like that, naked, hair loose, eyes closed, offering her vulnerability to her memories.

When she managed to tear herself away from the past, she got dressed, did her hair, and joined Iris and Théo in the sitting room.

"He's fallen asleep," the young woman whispered.

Jeanne went up to the cradle, beside the sofa. Two tiny fists framed the sweet little face of the child who was capturing a bit more of her heart every day.

"This is a special day," she said quietly, sitting down. "It's the first anniversary of Pierre's death. I've never managed to before, but today I want to tell you about it."

And so Jeanne told them. About the suitcase, the motorhome trip, the blue sky, Pierre going out to buy some bread, the crowd, the cardiac massage, the ambulance, the final look. She told of the last moments of a life that's over, in a breath, eyes cast towards yesterday. She didn't see Théo blanching. She didn't see Iris putting her hand over her mouth.

Throughout our lives, we encounter thousands of people. Invisible links are formed between them and us, and make us the individuals we are. Some links are fleeting, others enduring, all influence our existence. From the person we exchange a few words with while waiting in line, to the one we choose to share some of our life with. There are the faces we pass by and those that remain. There are the faces we choose, and those that impose themselves. There are the faces we forget and those that leave an impression on us. There are the faces we come across several times.

Iris. Théo. Last June 15.

Théo remembers Nathalie's cry. "The customer's had a bad turn!" Théo had only been working at the bakery for a few days. Quickly summoning what he'd learnt at first-aid training, he'd rushed outside and given cardiac massage to the man lying on the pavement.

Iris remembered the crowd. Some passers-by had gathered around someone who had fallen to the ground. She was on her way to a job interview at an agency for care workers. She'd asked if someone had called for an ambulance, no one had replied. She'd done so herself.

Both of them remembered the lady who had come running, barefoot on the pavement. They had left the scene as soon as the ambulance had arrived, remembering her tears, but not her face.

Jeanne listened to them telling her how their paths had already crossed. How, without knowing it, they were linked. How terribly sorry they were that they hadn't been able to save him.

She remained silent for a long while, taking that information in, wondering at life's mysterious ways, gazing at those faces that she had come across without seeing them, and then she smiled.

"You didn't save him, but you did save me."

Acknowledgments

When I started writing this novel, I was sure of just one thing: it would be about encounters. I'm convinced that the people we come across throughout our lives influence our trajectories. Which is why, as I write these acknowledgments, I think of those encounters that, day after day, make me the woman and novelist that I am.

Thank you to my family—my foundation, my plinth, my pillars, my oxygen: my children and my husband, who share my days, my nights, and my heart. My mother, my father, my sister, my nephew, my niece, my grandparents, my aunts, and my uncles, who are so important.

Thank you to my friends—my certainties: Sophie, Cynthia, and Serena, my dear Bertitis, who proved to me that friendship, the true sort, could just happen to us at any age. Marine, Gaëlle, Baptiste, Justine, Yannis, and Faustine, for being by my side for such a long time.

Thank you to those who accepted to reread my novel before it reached you, and allowed me, through their comments, to improve it: Arnold, Muriel, Serena Giuliano, Sophie Rouvier, Cynthia Kafka, Baptiste Beaulieu, Constance Trapenard, Audrey, Marie Vareille, Michael Palmeira, Sophie Bordelais, Florence Prévoteau, Marine Climent, and Camille Anseaume.

Infinite thanks to Fabien, aka Grand Corps Malade, who, in addition to being a talented artist, is a generous man who allowed me to use his magnificent title, "Il nous restera ça" [*All That Remains*]. I encourage you all to listen to his albums, and particularly the one with that title. The song "Pocahontas" has made me cry every time I've listened to it, for years.

Thank you to my editor, Alexandrine Duhin, for her unfailing presence and her words that can get me back on the road when I stall. Thank you to Sophie de Closets for her trust, her good eye, and her friendship.

Thank you to all those who work behind the scenes so that the words typed on my keyboard turn into the book in your hands, and with whom, in many cases, some lovely links have been forged: At Fayard: Jérôme Laissus, Sophie Hogg-Grandjean, Katy Fenech, Laurent Bertail, Carole Saudejaud, Catherine Bourgey, Éléonore Delair, Florian Madisclaire, Pauline Duval, Romain Fournier, Pauline Faure, Ariane Foubert, Véronique Héron, Iris Neron-Bancel, Florence Ameline, Clémence Gueudré, Anne Schuliar, Delphine Pannetier, and Martine Thibet.

At Livre de Poche: Béatrice Duval, Audrey Petit, Zoé Niewdanski, Sylvie Navellou, Claire Lauxerrois, Anne Bouissy, Florence Mas, Dominique Laude, William Koenig, Bénédicte Beaujouan, and Antoinette Bouvier. And all the sales representatives, who work so hard to bring the books to you.

Thank you to the bookshops, which, despite recent testing times, are still passionate about building bridges between authors and readers.

Thank you to Valérie Renaud for dedicating so much time in search of a wonderful cover.

Thank you to Lorraine Fouchet and Valérie Perrin, two lovely encounters at various book fairs.

Thank you to the bloggers who pass on their love of the books so generously.

Thank you to Jean-Jacques Goldman for allowing me to quote his words, a little nod to my first book, *Le Premier Jour du reste de ma vie*, in which he played an important part.

And immense, profound, sincere thanks to you, dear readers. I don't necessarily know your faces, your voices, very often we've never met, or even corresponded. And yet you are one of my loveliest encounters. Thank you for your invisible presence that means so much to me.

Europa Editions UK

Read the World

Literary fiction, popular fiction, narrative non-fiction,
travel, memoir, world noir

Building bridges between cultures with the finest writing from around the world.

Ahmet Altan, Peter Cameron, Andrea Camilleri, Catherine Chidgey,
Sandrine Collette, Christelle Dabos, Donatella Di Pietrantonio, Négar Djavadi,
Deborah Eisenberg, Elena Ferrante, Lillian Fishman, Anna Gavalda,
Saleem Haddad, James Hannaham, Jean-Claude Izzo, Maki Kashimada,
Nicola Lagioia, Alexandra Lapierre, Grant Morrison, Ondjaki, Valérie Perrin,
Christopher Prendergast, Eric-Emmanuel Schmitt, Domenico Starnone,
Esther Yi, Charles Yu

Acts of Service, *Didn't Nobody Give a Shit What Happened to Carlotta*,
Ferocity, *Fifteen Wild Decembers*, *Fresh Water for Flowers*, *Lambda*,
Love in the Days of Rebellion, *My Brilliant Friend*, *Remote Sympathy*,
Sleeping Among Sheep Under a Starry Sky, *Total Chaos*, *Transparent City*,
What Happens at Night, *A Winter's Promise*

Europa Editions was founded by Sandro Ferri and Sandra Ozzola,
the owners of the Rome-based publishing house Edizioni E/O.

Europa Editions UK is an independent trade publisher
based in London.

www.europaeditions.co.uk

Follow us at . . .
Twitter: @EuropaEdUK
Instagram: @EuropaEditionsUK
TikTok: @EuropaEditionsUK